ADDENDUM TO CONTRACT #1099 BETWEEN WILLIAM HARDISON AND KATHRYN O'CONNOR

1. Both parties will ignore the sparks that ignite between them whenever they are in a room together.

2. They will forget the soul-touching kisses they have already exchanged and never engage in such activities again.

3. If, after all this, either party falls in love with the other party to this contract…well, that is *their* problem, and this office shall not be held responsible in any way.

Signed: *William H. Hardison*

William H. Hardison

Signed: *Kathryn O'Connor*

Kathryn O'Connor

Dear Reader,

Silhouette Romance is proud to usher in the year with *two* exciting new promotions! LOVING THE BOSS is a six-book series, launching this month and ending in June, about office romances leading to happily-ever-afters. In the premiere title, *The Boss and the Beauty*, by award-winning author Donna Clayton, a prim personal assistant wows her jaded, workaholic boss when she has a Cinderella makeover....

You've asked for more family-centered stories, so we created FAMILY MATTERS, an ongoing promotion with a special flash. The launch title, *Family by the Bunch* from popular Special Edition author Amy Frazier, pairs a rancher in want of a family with a spirited social worker...and *five* adorable orphans.

Also available are more of the authors you love, and the miniseries you've come to cherish. Kia Cochrane's emotional Romance debut, *A Rugged Ranchin' Dad*, beautifully captures the essence of FABULOUS FATHERS. Star author Judy Christenberry unveils her sibling-connected miniseries LUCKY CHARM SISTERS with *Marry Me, Kate*, an unforgettable marriage-of-convenience tale. *Granted: A Family for Baby* is the latest of Carol Grace's BEST-KEPT WISHES miniseries. And COWBOYS TO THE RESCUE, the heartwarming Western saga by rising star Martha Shields, continues with *The Million-Dollar Cowboy*.

Enjoy this month's offerings, and look forward to more spectacular stories coming each month from Silhouette Romance!

Happy New Year!

Mary-Theresa Hussey

Mary-Theresa Hussey
Senior Editor, Silhouette Romance

Please address questions and book requests to:
Silhouette Reader Service
U.S.: 3010 Walden Ave., P.O. Box 1325, Buffalo, NY 14269
Canadian: P.O. Box 609, Fort Erie, Ont. L2A 5X3

JUDY CHRISTENBERRY

MARRY ME, KATE

Published by Silhouette Books

America's Publisher of Contemporary Romance

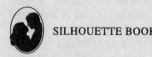

SILHOUETTE BOOKS

ISBN 0-373-19344-0

MARRY ME, KATE

Copyright © 1999 by Judy Christenberry

Printed in U.S.A.

Books by Judy Christenberry

Silhouette Romance

The Nine-Month Bride #1324
*Marry Me, Kate #1343

* Lucky Charm Sisters

JUDY CHRISTENBERRY

has been writing romances for fifteen years because she loves happy endings as much as her readers. She's a best-selling writer for Harlequin American Romance, but she has a long love of traditional romances and is delighted to tell a story that brings those elements to the reader. Judy recently quit teaching French and devotes her time to writing. She hopes readers have as much fun reading her stories as she does writing them. She spends her spare time reading, watching her favorite sports teams and keeping track of her two daughters. Judy's a native Texan, living in Plano, a suburb of Dallas.

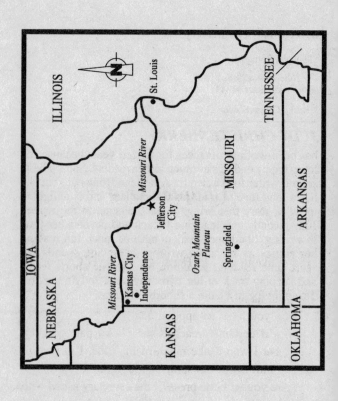

Chapter One

"I'd like to see Mr. Hardison," Kate O'Connor announced calmly to the efficient-looking woman behind the large desk.

"Do you have an appointment?"

They'd certainly reached the sticky part quickly. "No, but I won't take much of his time. I'm here to talk to him about the sponsor program."

"Are you with the press?" the secretary asked with a frown, flipping the pages of her calendar.

Kate wanted to say yes, but her innate honesty wouldn't let her. "No."

"Then why do you want to speak to Mr. Hardison?"

"I'd prefer to give my explanation to him," Kate returned, her spine stiffening with resentment at the woman's attitude. *Careful*, she warned herself. She mustn't let her temper do her in. She needed to subdue it just as she'd subdued her red hair this morning, pinning it into a sedate French roll.

"I can give you ten minutes next month."

Next month wouldn't do. She was too close to going under. "I need to see him now."

"Sorry." The word was accompanied by a superior smile that made control of her temper difficult. Without another word, Kate walked out of the deeply carpeted office. Once the door had closed behind her, she sank against the wall, her shaking knees and aching heart unable to continue.

It had been two months since her father's death. Two difficult months. She'd discovered the diner her father had run for years had been losing money the past twelve months and, along with his medical bills, had almost exhausted her father's savings. She'd come up with a plan to keep the diner, but she needed an infusion of capital. Her sister Maggie had offered *her* savings, even though she didn't want to keep the diner, but Kate couldn't take Maggie's money.

A smile lit her face. Pop always said Maggie was a changeling because of her cautiousness. But she was financially solvent, the only one in the family. Their half sister Susan, only recently discovered by Kate and Maggie, was trying to raise two half siblings on her own. She certainly couldn't invest in Kate's idea.

Besides, Kate felt it was her job, as oldest in the family, to take care of her sisters. Not the other way around. And she was determined to do so. When she'd turned to the banks, however, they wouldn't offer her much without better collateral.

She'd been desperate when an article in the newspaper had caught her attention. The CEO of Hardison Enterprises had begun a sponsoring program for small businesses.

Without waiting for second thoughts, she'd dressed in her only business suit, a bright blue, Parisian-designed outfit that showed off her curves, and had come to see Mr. Hardison at once. It turned out she needn't have called at all since she couldn't see him *with* an appointment until next month.

The door behind her opened and she heard the snooty secretary say, "I'll have it for you in fifteen minutes, Mr. Hardison."

Then, as the door closed, Kate watched the back of the woman as she hurried down the hall away from her.

Leaving the CEO unguarded.

I know you always warned me about being impulsive, Pop, but I've got to go for it.

She quietly opened the door and slipped back into the outer office. Staring at the door to the forbidden sanctum across the room, she briefly wondered if she had the nerve to just walk in.

She grinned. Pop always said she had more nerve than sense. She'd never proved him wrong. It wouldn't happen now. She pushed away from the wall, charged across the room and opened the inner office door.

Her first surprise when she caught sight of the man behind the desk was his age. If pressed, she'd guess him to be thirty, give or take a couple of years. Had she gotten the wrong office? This man appeared too young to be the head of Hardison Enterprises. And somehow she hadn't pictured Mr. Hardison as being so...sexy.

Then he stood. His tall, lean frame only increased the intimidation she felt as she looked at him. On a lesser man, she would've called his expression a glare. On him, the look threatened bodily harm to anyone who bothered him.

"Mr. Hardison?"

"Who are you?" he snapped.

Bingo. She had the right office.

"My name is Kathryn O'Connor. I need to talk to you about the sponsor program."

"Are you a reporter?" His voice was harsh.

What was it with these people? Were their lives so exciting that they were constantly pursued by the press?

"No. But I—"

"Then get out." He sat back down and turned his attention to a pile of papers on his desk.

Kate stood there, wondering what her next move should be. She wasn't about to give up but—

"I told you to leave." He didn't even look up.

"Not before I talk to you. I want to be considered for the sponsor program."

He covered his handsome face with one hand before looking at her. "*That's* what you want? Forget it."

"Wait a minute. I'd be a good risk," she protested, moving closer to his desk.

"Then go to a bank." He turned his attention back to his paperwork.

"They won't loan me enough money."

"Lady, there are no free rides, even for someone who looks like you." His gaze roved over her and she felt her cheeks heat up.

"I'm not asking for a free ride," she returned, her voice reflecting her anger at his accusation.

"That's what they all say."

She moved over next to the desk, as irritated by the way he ignored her as she was by his words.

"At least listen to me," she pleaded.

"Out," he replied calmly, making notes on a letter.

Something snapped in Kate, to be treated this way after the struggle she'd had. She smashed her hand down on top of the letter. "You have to listen to me."

Slowly William Hardison lifted his gaze from the letter to stare at hazel eyes, their luminous quality enhanced by her anger.

It wasn't her beauty that caught his attention. He was constantly in the company of beautiful women.

No, it was her firm little chin, the determined glint in her eyes. He sighed. He'd already faced a determined woman this morning.

His mother.

She'd been on his case again, wanting him to promise to attend the reception this evening for society's finest. And to escort her newest candidate for the role of Mrs. William Hardison. His mother never stopped trying to manipulate, cajole or force him into doing what she wanted. Just as she had his father.

James Hardison had married later than most men. Almost forty, he'd fallen head over heels for Miriam Esters. After finally agreeing to marry the wealthy businessman, she'd led him around by the nose for the rest of his life.

It wouldn't have bothered Will so much if she'd made his dad happy. But she'd never let him believe she loved him, and she'd never been satisfied with the gifts he'd showered on her.

As much as he'd loved his father, Will had despised James's weakness for his mother.

After a few unfortunate forays into the romance arena himself, Will had come to the conclusion that most women were like his mother. Best left alone.

Now, as the attractive young lady smashed her hand down on the letter he was reading, he realized that, like his mother, she wasn't going to go away without a fight.

He noticed her nails: clean, neatly trimmed, instead of the long red claws his mother and all her friends sported. Probably meant she wouldn't try to scratch his eyes out. At least he hoped not.

"Miss…whatever your name is, I believe I asked you to leave." He spoke in measured tones, hoping to defuse the situation.

"I suppose people always do exactly what you ask?" she demanded.

"Well," he said consideringly, a faint smile on his lips, "it *is* my office."

"All I'm asking is for you to hear me out! I'm a perfect candidate for your sponsorship." In her agitation, her hair was escaping from its pins, curly strands framing her face.

"How would you know the perfect candidate?"

"I read about Paul Jones in the paper."

"And you want to be the next Paul Jones?" he asked, his voice taking on a sharp edge as he looked at her more closely. Did she realize Paul Jones had been a con artist? Was she one, also?

"Yes!"

"No way in hell, lady. Now, get out of my office or I'll call security." He wasn't about to get himself in another mess like the one with Paul Jones. The man had lied and cheated and threatened blackmail. So much for Will's philanthropical efforts.

"Why won't you listen to me?" she cried out. "Is it because I'm a woman? Are you one of those men who believe women are incapable of counting above ten?"

He gave her his most cynical smile. "The women I know are quite capable of counting millions, especially if it's someone else's millions."

Her chin thrust forward and her eyes narrowed. "I'm only asking to be heard. I'm not trying to steal from you."

"Look, our sponsorship program has been suspended pending evaluation, so you're wasting your time."

"No!" she snapped, as if it were her decision. "No, no, no!"

He grinned. How his mother would hate this woman, so demanding, argumentative, determined. She was exactly the opposite of those sweet-smelling, soft creatures whose hearts were made of iron.

In fact, if he chose a wife like this lady, his mother would probably wash her hands of him in despair.

As his hand reached for the phone to call security,

he halted in midair. A ridiculous thought—but intriguing. He shot a look at her ring finger. Bare.

"Are you married?" he asked.

For the first time since she'd entered his office, she drew back. Only inches, but a definite retreat.

"Why?"

"I want to know."

She hesitated but finally answered, "No."

"I will listen to your pitch tonight. Write down your address," he ordered, shoving a piece of paper and a pen across his desk, "and I'll pick you up at eight. It's formal."

"What's formal?" she asked, her voice wary. She hadn't picked up the pen yet, and he wondered just how strong her determination was. She might save him from his bizarre idea if she weakened.

"I have to attend a reception this evening. It's the only time I can give you. Take it or leave it."

She stared at him and he calmly waited for her decision. He'd always been a gambler. But he'd never taken such a personal risk before.

She reached out for the pen and paper and wrote down an address. He took it from her and nodded as he folded it and put it into his top pocket. "Eight o'clock." Without another word he returned to his perusal of the letter. Even as she walked to his office door, he'd lost himself in the new project he was working on.

Will put his Jaguar in Park and pulled the piece of paper from his tux jacket pocket: 1205 Wornall Avenue. He slowly lifted his gaze to the monstrosity in

front of him. The Lucky Charm Diner—an old trolley
car, painted a pea green, though half the paint had
peeled off, set at the edge of the small parking lot.
The sign on top of it was covered with graffiti, making its name almost unreadable.

She couldn't live here. The woman he'd seen this
morning, Kathryn O'Connor, in that elegant blue suit,
couldn't live in a diner. If she did, his plan would not
only upset his mother, but it might also give her a
heart attack.

Maybe Miss O'Connor just wanted to meet him
here. She hadn't seemed the cautious type, though
these days any woman should be. But couldn't she
find a classier place to meet?

He shut off the engine and got out of the car. As
he stood there, adjusting his gold cuff links, a rattle-
trap old pickup pulled into one of the many empty
spaces. Without even a glance in his direction, two
grizzled men in coveralls got out and entered the
diner.

With a shrug, Will followed them.

He surveyed the small eatery, noting the faded ta-
bletops, their green color matching the outside paint,
the patched and uneven floor, the close quarters.
Clearly a down-and-out café. Its name had certainly
not been lucky for the owner.

Clearing his throat, he waited for the only em-
ployee in sight, a frizzy-haired, middle-aged woman,
to acknowledge him.

"Just come on in and park yourself, honey. We're
not formal here." Even as she greeted him, she was

pouring coffee for the two men who had preceded him.

"I'm looking for Miss Kathryn O'Connor," he explained crisply, trying to hold back his distaste.

The woman paused and giggled, her gaze sweeping over him. "Oh! You must be the gentleman she said would be coming. Kate!" she called in gargantuan tones. "He's here."

Will barely stopped himself from shaking his head in amazement. He couldn't have chosen a better place to shock his mother if he'd tried. The picture of her entering this establishment, in her fur and pearls, almost made him burst out laughing.

The redhead appeared from a door to the side of the counter. The men drinking their coffee put down their cups and clapped and whistled, jerking Will from his thoughts.

She was wearing a little black dress, cut low in front, displaying her charms, and slit to the thigh on one side. Sheer black nylons led his eyes to the high heels that only emphasized all those curves.

His mouth suddenly dry, he cleared his throat again and muttered, "Good evening, Miss O'Connor."

Seemingly unaffected by his appearance, she replied, "Hello, Mr. Hardison. Are you ready?"

"Hey, Kate, where you going, all duded up?" a member of their audience called out.

Will frowned in his direction but waited for the woman to answer.

"This is a business meeting, Larry."

"Whooeee! I think I'm going into business!" the man whooped as all the others laughed.

Will's soon-to-be date laughed along with the men, but he didn't. "Miss O'Connor, this is a formal affair," he said.

"This is as dressy as I come, Mr. Hardison. I haven't frequented formal occasions lately."

His gaze briefly roamed the diner before he said, "I can see." He hadn't intended his remark as a criticism but he saw the flash of anger in her green eyes.

"If I'll be too much of an embarrassment to you, we can have our meeting here and then you can proceed without me."

"Not at all, Miss O'Connor. After you." He was looking a gift horse in the mouth. Why worry about her embarrassment if she didn't? He'd never deliberately place any woman in such an awkward situation, but he'd warned her. It wasn't his fault she wasn't properly dressed.

After they were settled in the Jaguar and on their way, he said, "The man in there called you Kate."

"Yes."

"Ah. Do you mind if I call you Kate?"

She'd been staring straight ahead until now. Turning, she let one brow slip up in a fascinating manner. "Are we going to be informal, then?"

There was a challenge in the husky tones that made his gut clench. He didn't want to react to her, but her sexy apparel combined with her attractions would make any man sit up and take notice.

"I thought it might be a good idea—since we're going to be in each other's company all night."

"All night?"

Damn, she was making him sound like an adoles-

cent boy, stumbling through his first date. "Too lit-
eral, Miss O'Connor. I of course meant all evening.
Though when the evening *ends* will be your choice.
I'm a gentleman."

"Don't play word games with me, Mr. Hardison,"
she returned, her voice smooth and enveloping.
"Given my choice, we would've had our meeting in
your office."

He breathed deeply and inhaled her perfume. His
gaze swept up her leg, following the slit that teased
him with a glimpse of a firm thigh.

"Tell me about the project you think would be perfect for Hardison Industries's entrepreneurial program." If he didn't change the subject and stop thinking about how the evening might end, he was going
to embarrass himself.

"Can't you guess?"

Such a strange answer brought his gaze back to her.
"I beg your pardon?"

"The light's turned green," she murmured just as
the car behind him sounded its horn.

Embarrassed, he stomped on the accelerator and the
tires squealed as he roared through the intersection.
Feeling like a teenager, he tried to bring himself under
control.

"What did you mean?" he finally asked.

"You've already seen my project."

He frowned. He really wasn't interested in discussing business right now. His plans were more important. All he'd hoped to do was distract his mind from
the urges that were overtaking him every time he
looked at her. But now she'd caught his attention.

"I don't know what you're talking about. All I've seen is you."

"Not unless you walked inside the diner with your eyes closed."

"Walked inside—" He broke off and stared at her again in horror. "You can't mean—"

"Watch out!" she shrieked and grabbed the steering wheel to help him avoid a parked car.

He turned back to the road, keeping his gaze firmly fixed in front of him, as he fought through the shock. "You're saying The—The Lucky Charm is your project? You've got to be kidding!"

Chapter Two

Kate wasn't pleased with the shock in his voice. The man was a snob, just like her Aunt Lorraine, who hated the diner. Anger warred with despair. She *needed* his money. Desperately. Otherwise, she would never have agreed to have a business discussion in a social setting.

"I'm quite serious, Mr. Hardison. I have figures to show you that support my intentions."

He pulled into a parking lot that encircled the Nelson-Atkins Museum of Art and stopped by the front door where a valet waited to park his car. It wasn't until he reached her side after circling the vehicle that he responded.

"Either I'm thinking of a different kind of figure or they don't amount to much, Kate. Because I don't see where you could've hidden any more of your figure wearing that dress."

The steamy stare that swept her from her toes to

her shoulders, or perhaps a little below her shoulders, told Kate there wasn't much hope for a business discussion. This man had his mind on other things.

Stiffening her shoulders, she raised her chin and waited until his gaze finally left her breasts. "I'm asking for a loan, Mr. Hardison, not selling myself. A business discussion is what I want, not…not a seduction."

Though his cheeks reddened, he looked down his nose at her as if she were a common bug that happened to intrude in his path. "Of course. That's my intention also."

He took her arm, a touch that Kate felt all over, and led her toward the door, immediately opened by an attendant. Standing just inside was a receiving line of gray-haired women dressed in elegant, floor-length gowns, adorned in diamonds and pearls. Their escorts wore tuxedos, like Hardison's.

Kate hid an inner groan beneath a smile. She'd occasionally attended such social events with her aunt Lorraine. And hated every minute of them.

The first lady stared at her in horror, as if unable to believe her eyes, and Kate quickly glanced down her person, afraid something was amiss. Her short black dress was certainly less formal than their gowns, but she was decently covered.

When she raised her gaze, she saw her escort bend over and kiss the woman's cheek.

"Evening, Mother. I'd like you to meet Kate O'Connor. She works at The Lucky Charm Diner on Wornall Avenue."

The woman's face paled, and she wavered on her

high heels. Kate feared they'd be picking her up off the floor any minute. And wondered if William Hardison had intended that result with his invitation.

After all, it hadn't been necessary to mention the diner at all, much less make it sound as if she was working for minimum wage. Though minimum wage might be an increase in her income right now.

"I—I—how do you do?" the woman finally warbled, sounding as if she had a tickle in her throat.

"Fine, thank you, Mrs. Hardison." Kate pretended a lack of interest in the woman's distress, hoping she would understand that her accompanying the woman's son was an impersonal thing. "Your gown is lovely."

The woman's gaze trailed down Kate's figure, as if she intended to return the compliment, then thought better of it. "Thank you," she muttered and dropped Kate's hand.

The man next to Mrs. Hardison instantly grabbed Kate's fingers and lifted them to his lips. Kate wasn't fond of hand kissing, but having lived in France for four years, she wasn't stunned by his action. His devouring stare bothered her more.

"Absolutely stunning, Miss O'Connor. I hope you'll save me a dance. I'm Count Ryzinski."

She supposed his affected speech was meant to imply he was European, but Kate didn't believe it for a minute. She slipped her hand from his with no comment.

William Hardison's arm slid around her waist and he introduced her to the next dowager in line. Distracted by his touch much more than the count's kiss, Kate couldn't remember the woman's name.

Not that it mattered.

She wouldn't see any of them after tonight, whether she got her loan or not. Unless, of course, they became future customers.

Will kept his hand on Kate's waist, enjoying the feel of her. She might not be dressed as elegantly as the elite of Kansas City, but she shouted sex appeal.

And he was a healthy man.

The count, one of his mother's hangers-on, appeared to be healthy, too. Too much so. It irritated Will that the man had kissed Kate's hand, though it hadn't seemed to bother her.

As they continued down the receiving line, he discovered every man introduced to Kate was affected by her curvaceous figure.

He wanted to punch them all out.

As soon as they'd finished the introductions, he took her arm and pulled her in the direction of the serving tables. ''Let's get a drink.''

A waiter stepped in front of them with a tray. ''Champagne, sir?''

Will grabbed two glasses and handed one to Kate.

She calmly set it back down on the tray. With a smile to the waiter, she said, ''I'd prefer mineral water. Is it available?''

The waiter acted as if he'd been given a commission of greatness. ''I'll bring it to you personally, miss,'' he assured her, a hungry grin on his lips.

She thanked him and he hurried away, an almost

full tray in his grasp, ignoring the people who were waiting to be served.

"You're dangerous," Will murmured.

"I beg your pardon?"

"Try not to ask for any more favors. I'm afraid half the men in here will fall on their faces rushing to serve you." He noted the flash of anger in her eyes with satisfaction. The more off balance she felt, the more outrageous she'd behave.

And the more upset his mother would become.

"Will! Where have you been lately, buddy?" a male voice called out.

Will turned to see John Larabee, Jr., an old school chum, approaching. He shouldn't have been surprised. Jack had always chased the most beautiful women, and Kate was easily in that category.

"Hello, lovely lady," Jack added as he reached Will and Kate. He took Kate's hand in his and held it.

"Good evening," Kate said coolly and tugged on her hand.

"Let her go, Jack."

Both his companions stared at him, Kate with indignation in her gaze, and Jack with a considering look. However, Jack didn't bother to let go of Kate's hand.

Kate tugged on her hand again. When the man didn't immediately release it, she took Will's champagne out of his hand and calmly poured what was left down the front of Jack's tuxedo.

"Oh, I'm so sorry. How careless of me," she said, a sweet smile of concern on her lush lips.

Jack stared at his tuxedo in horror, but he also released Kate's hand. "You—you—that—" he sputtered, wiping his shirtfront and glaring at her at the same time.

Several people around them, apparently having watched the brief scenario, gave gasps of disapproval and moved to console Jack, a favorite with the elite of Kansas City.

"That was very rude, young lady," a blue-haired dowager snapped as her husband offered a handkerchief to Jack.

"Oh, I quite agree," Kate said calmly, "but you know how some men are. They just can't behave themselves." She smiled and then excused herself and moved toward the service table.

Will closed his gaping mouth, swallowed a chuckle and followed in Kate's wake. This evening was going to be more fun than he'd ever had before at one of his mother's events.

"A bit extreme, but effective," he whispered in Kate's ear as she looked over the hors d'oeuvres.

"Thank you," she replied calmly, never lifting her gaze from the table.

Just as he decided she'd earned her interview, his mother arrived, outrage on her face.

"William! Is it true? Did this—this woman pour champagne on Jack?"

Kate, holding a plate with various hors d'oeuvres on it, turned to look at his mother. "Is Jack a friend of yours, Mrs. Hardison? I hope he's not upset by my little accident. If he's concerned about the champagne staining—"

"Young woman! I heard it was no accident!" She turned so that Kate was facing her back and looked at Will. "I cannot believe you would bring such a social misfit to our gala!"

Will had hoped the young woman would disturb his mother, but he hadn't expected such a scene. Even so, it wasn't fair for Kate to be treated so harshly. Without even thinking, he leapfrogged several unexplained steps in his plan and circled Kate with his arm.

"Why wouldn't I bring her, Mother? Kate and I are to be married."

Several glasses crashed even as Miriam Hardison slumped to the floor in a dead faint.

The silence in the car was deafening as William Hardison drove Kate home. After his mother fainted, pandemonium had reigned. Kate had taken the opportunity to sample some of the hors d'oeuvres, knowing her departure was imminent.

Even as Mrs. Hardison regained consciousness, several dowagers remonstrated with the root of all the problems, William. Kate listened to their impassioned words as she watched her escort's expression. As his jaw squared, she stepped forward.

"William, dear, I'm ready to leave. Shall I call a taxi?" *As if she could afford such an extravagance.* "I'll understand if you want to stay with your mother."

At least he wasn't dumb, she decided with relief. His glare told her he got her message loud and clear. She was leaving, with or without him.

"No, I'll take you home." He turned to the slumped-over woman, her head resting on the count's shoulder, bravely sipping champagne. "Mother, I'm taking Kate home now. I'll call you tomorrow."

Without waiting for a response, he'd taken Kate's arm and strode from the museum.

She'd wondered if he'd explain, though she couldn't think of any explanation that would justify his behavior. She hated being used, especially to upset someone. She might not enjoy the company of society ladies, but she didn't wish them any harm.

When he drove in silence, offering nothing to account for his behavior, she silently said goodbye to her dream. After all, there hadn't been much hope anyway. They wouldn't sell the diner, but she'd have to take another job and save until she could carry out her goal.

Without the rude man beside her.

He pulled up to the diner and parked the car, then opened his door.

Kate didn't bother telling him it wasn't necessary to escort her to the door. He was the kind of man who wouldn't listen to reason. She'd already figured that out.

Of course, she was curious about what had made him agree to an interview in the first place. But it didn't matter. That possibility had gone the way of so many other plans.

"Good night, Mr. Hardison," she muttered as she reached for the front door of the diner.

He opened the door and then entered behind her.

She was suddenly grateful for the few customers lining the counter and the curious Madge.

"We haven't had our talk," Hardison said quietly.

She spun around to stare at him. "You never intended one, did you? After tonight's events, I assume your only interest in me was comic relief."

"I never expected…the situation deteriorated faster than I…I want to apologize for my mother's rudeness."

Kate stifled the gratitude she felt for his effort. "Very gracious, since *you* caused the problem."

"What are you talking about?"

"I'm not an idiot, Mr. Hardison. And I don't appreciate being used."

"I didn't—"

"Have a good time, hon?" Madge called, reminding Kate that every person in the diner was staring at them.

With a brief smile, Kate turned. "A lovely time, Madge. Is Paula working in the morning?"

"Yep, as usual."

"Well, I'll see you tomorrow afternoon." Without ever turning around to speak to her escort, Kate headed for the double doors that swung into the kitchen.

She'd only managed one step when a strong hand grabbed her arm.

"We haven't had our discussion."

"As I pointed out earlier," she said coldly, turning to glare at him, "I'm not an idiot. Whatever this evening was about, it wasn't business."

* * *

Kate O'Connor was right about one thing. She wasn't an idiot, Will decided as he admired her snapping hazel eyes and flushed cheeks. And she was a beauty.

And she'd more than proved his theory.

"I promise you I intend to discuss your, uh, business plans. I'll give you my full attention for one hour and you can show me those figures you said you had prepared." Not that he expected anything that would make a lick of business sense. Not if it had to do with the ramshackle diner.

She didn't grab the opportunity he offered. Instead she planted her hands on those slender hips that had drawn his gaze more than once and stared at him.

"Why?"

Of course she would ask. "Because I keep my word. You fulfilled your end of the bargain. Now it's my turn."

He found it fascinating to watch the changes in her expressive eyes as she considered his statement. Then she looked over her shoulder at their audience.

"Go on. Give him a chance," one customer, an older, unshaven man urged with a grin.

"Billy—" she began, then stopped. She turned back to stare at Will, her eyes narrowing.

He knew the instant she made up her mind and breathed a sigh of relief. Somehow, the thought of ending their acquaintance tonight bothered him more than he wanted to admit.

"All right, Mr. Hardison. I'll take your one hour. Come on." She spun on her heel and headed toward a back booth in the diner.

Will frowned. He didn't want to conduct business in the diner. With an audience. Hurrying after her, he said, "Don't you think we could find a better place for our discussion?"

Like her bedroom.

He immediately shut down that errant thought. Business. He needed to think about business. But it was hard when he was following her trim figure encased in tight black, her red hair sparking as it moved with her.

"No."

Brief and to the point. He'd already learned she was direct, so he shouldn't have been surprised. "Okay," he agreed with a resigned sigh and slid into the plastic and Formica booth opposite her.

From the small black purse she'd carried with her all evening, she withdrew several sheets of paper folded to fit inside.

Kate couldn't believe she'd been given a second chance. Drawing a deep breath, she began to outline her plan to rescue her father's diner.

"A catering firm?" the man opposite her asked in surprise. "I hate to mention such mundane things, but catering is a tough business, with a low profit margin. And even more important, it requires good cooking skills."

Did he think she was an idiot? "Of course it does. But since I trained in Paris, I think my cooking will be adequate."

"Paris, France?"

The surprise on his face was offensive. "No, Paris,

Texas! Really, Mr. Hardison, must you insult my intelligence? Of course, Paris, France. I worked there as *sous*-chef of Maxim's for the past three years."

"Maxim's?" he repeated. "But I ate there last November."

"And you haven't died from ptomaine poisoning yet? Amazing." She had to remind herself not to be sarcastic. Pop always warned her about her sharp tongue, but the man was driving her crazy.

"I didn't mean—the food was good. But you don't look like you—I mean, your appearance—I'm surprised." He finished with red cheeks, but his gaze had roved her face and body and it didn't take much interpretation to understand his meaning.

"So you think only ugly women learn to cook?"

"No, of course not, but—let's see those figures."

Though his resorting to business to get him out of his difficulties was amusing, she didn't bother to smile. Too much was at stake. But it didn't keep her from appreciating that she had him at a disadvantage.

"All right, here's what I'm hoping to do."

She forgot the earlier events of the evening, her disgust with her companion, the despair that had filled her as they'd driven back to the diner. Inside, the flickering hope that had driven her to William Hardison in the first place flamed high as she described her plan to restore the diner to its former glory.

Or to more than its former glory since she wasn't sure it had ever been a smart establishment. Her plans included a large expansion of the kitchen to enable her to mass produce hors d'oeuvres and meals for the catering. And, since the man had agreed to listen, she threw in the apartment she planned to add on for herself.

"You want to live here?" His glance around the diner wasn't admiring.

"I already live here. I'd like to have nicer accommodations."

His gaze whipped back to hers. "Where?"

"I beg your pardon?"

"Where do you live?"

"There's a room behind the kitchen."

"I want to see it."

Her eyebrows raised. She had no intention of showing him her bedroom. She wasn't ashamed of it, exactly, but it wasn't a showplace, either. Just a room with a small bed, some space for her to store her clothes and a lot of boxes holding some of her belongings and those of her father. It was none of his business.

"No, that's not necessary."

"I think it is."

"But, you see, Mr. Hardison," she said with a glacial smile, "I don't much care what you think about my living quarters. I only care about your business acumen, in regard to my plans."

"I think you have about as much chance of being successful as the Royals do of making the playoffs."

Her confidence took a nosedive. The Royals, the local pro baseball team, were halfway through their season with a .348 percent win record.

She stiffened her back and raised her chin. "I see. Well, thank you for listening." She started to slide out of the booth, hoping she could escape before her eyes allowed the tears filling them to overrun down her cheeks.

"But I will give you the money," he said as he took hold of her arm.

She froze. Surely she had not heard correctly. He'd just said she had almost no chance to make her plan work. Then in the next breath he'd offered her the money?

Collecting herself, she asked sedately, as if her heart were not thumping like a drum, "On what terms?"

The smile on his lips should've warned her. But she was thinking percent, payments, length of loan, escrow. He wasn't.

"My terms are that you marry me."

Chapter Three

She gasped, drawing in a deep breath as she pulled herself together. Finally, when she had control once more, she said coldly, "I believe I mentioned earlier that I'm not for sale, Mr. Hardison."

With a frown, he said, "You misunderstand me, Miss O'Connor. I don't mean a real marriage. And I do not have any...designs on your body. The marriage would be one of convenience—for both of us—and would only last one year. There would be a pre-nuptial agreement spelling out the terms with a generous reward to you should I break any of them."

Will watched her as she tried to understand his words. Admittedly his proposition was unusual. And if she couldn't read his mind, perhaps even acceptable. He'd almost choked as he'd promised he had no interest in touching her, loving her. Physically. Of course, he had no interest in any emotional commitment.

He'd learned about that mistake from watching his father's life.

But physically, the lady was a turn-on that would be hard to resist. But he would. Drawing a deep breath himself, he waited for her reaction.

"I don't understand."

"You met my mother this evening."

"Yes. And I don't appreciate what you did."

"What did I do? I introduced you. The only thing I did wrong was announce our engagement before I spoke to you, but I said those words to protect you. My mother can be quite vicious to people she doesn't consider…suitable."

"To protect me," she said, her gaze narrowing as she studied him.

Feeling like a first-grader who had lied to his teacher, he tried to keep his features smooth and unconcerned. "Yes."

"And your reason for the proposal? Another attempt to protect me?"

Her sarcasm shattered his pretense and his cheeks flushed. "Not exactly."

"Then explain."

He'd figured she would demand details. Carefully selecting the version he wanted to reveal, he said, "My mother is…an ambitious woman. She's been trying to force me into an advantageous marriage for several years."

"And you're not grown-up enough to say no?"

Her scornful look angered him. "Yes, I can say no. And *have,* repeatedly. That doesn't stop her from disrupting my life with her efforts."

She frowned but said nothing.

"I want some peace. I'm starting a new project that is going to take a lot of my concentration and greatly expand my holdings, and I want her to leave me alone."

"And you can't find anyone willing to marry you without making them a financial offer?" Kate quizzed him. "What's wrong with you?"

"There's nothing wrong with me," he snapped back, burned by her condemnation. "Just because I don't want—I'm not interested in marriage."

Suddenly her big hazel eyes grew even larger and she leaned forward, whispering, "You're gay?"

Exasperation made him slump against the plastic seat as he shook his head. "No, I'm not. Damn it, woman, why can't you just accept what I'm telling you?"

"Because it doesn't make sense. Why would any man tie himself legally to a woman if he doesn't want marriage?"

"To keep from being persecuted by his mother."

"And to embarrass her, pay her back, perhaps?"

Damn, damn, damn. No, she wasn't stupid. "You're not exactly the kind of woman my mother wants me to marry." He cleared his throat. "If I married a society type, my mother would expect me to become even more involved in the society life-style. I want less."

"So you thought you'd choose a weed to grow among the lilies, knowing everyone will hate her and avoid you."

He didn't like what she was saying, but he couldn't

deny at least some of it. "If the men you met tonight liked you any more, this diner would be overflowing." She raised one eyebrow but said nothing. "Besides, what do you care if they don't like you? You'd get your money to make your dream come true."

"We still haven't discussed payback terms."

He smiled, knowing she wouldn't have asked if she wasn't considering his plan just a little. "That's the beauty of the plan for you, Kate. If you meet the terms of the agreement, you don't owe me anything."

Her mouth dropped in surprise. "You mean—you mean the money is a gift?"

"Nope. You're providing a service, and I'm paying. One year of your life."

"But I can work on the diner, get started?"

"I want you to work on the diner, to be too busy for any socializing," he assured her, feeling victory within his grasp.

"And all I have to do is go through a legal ceremony?"

"And pretend that we have a normal marriage."

Kate felt her elation subside. "What does that entail?"

"Not much. A few public displays of affection, moving into my house. Things like that."

"But not your bedroom?" she demanded, wanting to be clear about his demands.

"Not my bedroom," he assured her.

She stared at him. His voice was firm, his gaze clear, but there was a small flicker there that made her hesitate. That and the looks he'd given her this evening. Could she trust him?

Excitement filled her as she thought about finishing the year with her plans intact, debt-free. The possibility of succeeding was greatly enhanced if she had no loans. Maggie hadn't believed she could pull it off.

"All right," she said abruptly, looking him in the eye. "Have your lawyer draw up the papers. If everything is as you say, I'll agree."

What have I done?

That panicky question was lying in wait when Kate opened her eyes the next morning. She'd tossed and turned most of the night and felt more exhausted this morning than she had when she fell into bed.

Of course, five-thirty came early every morning, but she had no choice. Usually she hit the sack early, knowing the demands of the diner. Someday, she'd be able to hire someone else to share the burden of the cooking. Right now, she handled the eighteen-hour shift by cooking extra amounts and freezing them for when she couldn't be there, leaving her two waitresses to warm up the specials.

Thinking about the future brought her right back to the weird evening she'd suffered through. And the possibilities it offered. She had to call Maggie.

Rolling over, she reached for the phone and dialed her sister's number. "Maggie? Are you awake?"

Her sister growled into the phone. "The sun isn't up."

"I know. But I had to tell you. I've found someone to give me the money for the diner!"

Ever practical, Maggie got right to the point. "What do you have to do in return?"

Kate tried several ways of answering, but nothing came out. It wasn't easy to explain.

Maggie's voice tightened. "Kate? What's wrong?"

"Nothing," she hurriedly said. Maggie was younger by two years, but she'd always been the responsible one, the one to come along behind Kate and tidy up her messes.

"Then why haven't you answered my question?"

"Because it's hard to explain. It's—it's a personal services contract." That sounded like a polite way to categorize their agreement.

"Kate! You're not—"

"No!" Kate returned at once, understanding her sister's misapprehension from her tone of voice. Then she rethought her answer. "I'm going to—to marry the man for one year. A platonic marriage. Strictly business."

"Has he seen you?"

"Yes, of course he has."

"Then don't do it." With an exasperated sigh, Maggie added, "No man could marry you and keep it platonic…unless he's gay, of course. Is he?"

Kate let her thoughts travel over the sexy image of William Hardison in a tux. With a sigh, she admitted, "No, he's not."

"I don't like this, Kate."

"I know, Maggie, but I have to do it. For Pop. I know you don't like the idea—"

"I just don't think—never mind. I know it's important for you to keep the diner. But I don't want you to get hurt.''

"I won't. It's all going to be spelled out in an agreement. And I'll be able to make a good living. Maybe I can even help Susan some."

"If she'll let you. I've tried, but she's too proud. She won't let me do much."

"But that's the beauty of my plan, Maggie. She'll be part-owner. Both of you will. If I make any profits, you two will get your share."

Maggie, ever supportive, didn't voice her doubts, though Kate knew she had them. "Good. Have Tori look at the contract before you sign it."

Kate smiled. She'd known Maggie would be practical. "You're right. I'll call her."

After saying goodbye to her sister, she added to her list of things to do a call to Victoria Herring, a longtime friend who was an attorney. And Susan. She deserved to hear the good news, too. Maggie and Kate loved their new sister, but they found her as stubborn as either of them. She refused any offers of money to help her raise her siblings.

And without a debt overhead, Kate could offer real profit. She turned to the most entertaining of her plans, new menus. Catering offerings. What she'd tasted at the party at the museum last night wouldn't be hard to beat. She'd need an entrée, of course, to society, someone to lend her support.

She almost slipped in the shower as she realized the added benefit to marrying William Hardison. Of course! *He* would be her entrée. She'd been concentrating on the financial aspects of their agreement, but there was more to be gained from their liaison.

Frowning, she remembered his hope that she would keep him from the necessity of social engagements. Fine. That's what she would do. She would be working, anyway, if her ideas worked out. No one would expect her husband to accompany her on catering jobs.

Having nicely set him aside from her plans, Kate dressed and headed for the diner's kitchen, ready to start her day, hope riding high.

When Will reached his office the next morning, his secretary handed him a stack of messages from his mother. He'd turned off the ringer on his phone when he'd gotten home last night. He knew his mother would call and he didn't want to talk with her until he could present her with a fait accompli.

"She's already called three times, Mr. Hardison. I assured her you would be in shortly."

"And I am. But I don't want to talk to her just yet. If she calls again, tell her I'll be in touch by this evening, but whatever you do, don't put her through. And get Charles Wilson on the phone for me."

He'd barely sat down at his desk when his secretary buzzed him to pick up the phone.

After his greeting, his attorney asked, "Will? What's up, guy? I hear you caused a ruckus at last night's party."

"Maybe. Listen, I need some fast work. Can you clear your morning and get right over here?"

"Problem?"

Charles was not only a friend, but also an efficient, knowledgeable lawyer. He didn't waste time with protests.

''Not really. More of an agreement that will free me from problems, but it's…personal.''

Knowing his words would intrigue the other man, Will smiled as Charles gave him his assurance he'd be right over and hung up the phone.

Then he pulled the legal-size pad from his brief-case. Last night, when he'd been unable to go to sleep right away, he'd made a list of his requirements for the agreement. Now he wanted to review them. It wouldn't do to be careless. If he left a loophole, Miss Kate O'Connor could take him to the cleaners for a healthy reward.

She wouldn't do that. He dismissed that unbidden thought with a cynicism borne of living with a greedy woman—his mother. She had dared many things he would have thought beyond a woman who loved her husband, as she'd always professed to do.

Better to concentrate on the legalities. If he didn't leave any options for Miss O'Connor, then he wouldn't have to rely on a generous heart that he wasn't sure existed.

Charles stared at him.

''You want to do what?''

''Weren't you listening? I just explained it, Charles. It's not that complicated for a legal mind like yours.''

''Complicated? No. Stupid, yes.''

"Why? I thought you'd be pleased. I've covered every eventuality."

"What does this woman look like?"

Charles's unexpected question shook Will. "Why?"

"I heard she was a knockout. A redheaded bombshell." Charles's gaze remained fixed on Will.

How could he deny Charles's description? Even thinking about the way Kate had looked last night, the response from the other men, hell, from him, made denial impossible. "You heard right," he admitted tersely.

"And you want to put in the contract that if you have sex, even consensual sex, she gets half of everything?" Charles's voice rose higher with each word.

"Don't you have any faith in my self-control?" Will asked, glaring at his friend.

"Not unless you're no longer male. Proximity, legality and sex appeal don't promote abstinence when they're combined. It would be too easy to let yourself believe she cares about you when your hormones are in overdrive."

"Well, maybe I'll hang a copy of our agreement over my bed so I can't forget." Or a picture of his mother. Either one would be a reminder that women are out for what they can get…and nothing more.

"Man, you are crazy," Charles returned. "Don't you want to take some time to think about this—this contract?"

"Nope. She might change her mind." Will was afraid Kate might decide he wasn't offering enough and up her demands. "Can you have the contract ready by four this afternoon?"

"Four?" Charles exploded. "You've got to be kidding! This kind of contract is new to me. I've got to check out precedents, confirm legal opinions, word it exactly so as not to—"

"Just write it in plain English, Charles. Not that gobbledygook you lawyers use."

"That gobbledygook, as you call it, is what protects you from lawsuits. We won that suit filed by the last small businessman you sponsored because of it."

"This contract is personal. And I'm going to abide by my part of it, so we don't have to worry about *that* clause coming into play."

"You've taken up monkdom? Become a eunuch?"

"No, but I'm not an animal. If I have an itch, I'll find another way to scratch it, okay? She's not the only beautiful woman in the world."

"So you want me to make it clear that fidelity is not a requirement?"

"Man, does that sound crass or what? Surely we don't have to spell that kind of thing out?"

"The more we spell out, the less likely you'll find yourself in court trying to hang on to your company. And be sure she has legal representation present. We don't want her claiming we misled her."

Charles's stern look didn't impress Will all that much, but the thought of losing the company he'd inherited from his father and nourished and pushed into a large corporation did.

"Okay, put in whatever you have to. Then meet

me at The Lucky Charm Diner on Wornall Avenue at four o'clock, multiple copies in hand.''

Without protesting again, Charles strode from the office, muttering under his breath. Will figured he was already writing his opening paragraph of the agreement in his mind. Charles was nothing if not efficient.

Only occasionally did the hard, cold reality of all the aspects of her agreement impose on Kate's active brain that day. She let her spirits soar as she thought about the new decor of the diner, the new equipment, the opportunity to expand her culinary repertoire beyond chili, bacon and eggs, and hamburgers.

And maybe the opportunity to provide for her family, as Pop would have done.

She was so lost in her dreams, it was a shock to answer the phone and hear William Hardison's voice on the line.

''My lawyer is going to meet me at the diner at four o'clock with the agreement ready for signing.''

She checked her watch. ''But it's three o'clock now.''

''Yes, and you'll need a lawyer present.''

Nothing else. No apology for the short notice, no offer to meet at another time. The man was a definite autocrat.

''Okay.'' She could be as terse as he.

''I'll see you then.''

He left no time for her response. As she opened her mouth, the dial tone sounded in her ear. She slammed the receiver down in irritation. If he thought he was going to steamroll her, he had another think coming. She…and her lawyer…would read every word, study every comma, before she signed any legal document.

Since she'd already talked to Tori, she only had to let her know the time of the meeting, and listen to her complaints about short notice. But she knew Tori would be there.

Forty-five minutes later, her friend rushed through the door of the diner. "I'm here, but I left a disaster at the office. This had better be a good deal for you."

Kate hugged her friend. "Thanks. You know it is. I'm going to achieve my dream."

"Maggie says it's your folly. Have you told me all the details?"

"I think so. But that's why I need you here. They might slip in something else."

"I can't think of anything crazier than what you've already agreed to." Tori drew a deep breath and asked again. "Are you sure you want to do this?"

Just as she finished asking her question, the bell over the door rang and two men in suits headed in their direction.

"They're here," Kate explained, suddenly filled with panic.

Tori looked over her shoulder at the two men as they arrived at the table, then turned to stare at Kate.

It wasn't hard to read her friend's reaction. Both men could've been models in *GQ,* except they had a stamp of life experiences that added a few attractive wrinkles, a little more sex appeal.

Clearing her throat, Kate rose from the booth, Tori immediately joining her.

"Kate," her soon-to-be husband began, "May I present my lawyer, Charles Wilson? He's with Wilson, Stroud, Barkley and Wilson."

"How do you do? This is Victoria Herring, my attorney. She's with Linley, Carroll & Thompson." There, she thought in relief, tit for tat. Both law firms were well established in Kansas City. She was glad Maggie had thought of Tori.

"I'm pleased that you were able to find representation so quickly, Miss O'Connor," the handsome attorney said. "That way we'll all agree that there were no attempts to deceive."

"Of course," Tori agreed smoothly, nodding at the man.

Kate didn't care what the attorney or her prospective groom thought. She wanted to get on with her plans.

"Shall we be seated?" Mr. Wilson suggested, gesturing to the booth they'd just vacated. "In fact, I'd like to order a cup of coffee. It's been a long day already."

Kate waved to Madge for service. While she was doing so, Tori and her counterpart slid into the booth on the same side. Kate had been counting on Tori moving to sit beside her, allowing her to keep her distance from the man who was turning her world upside down.

"Uh, Tori, shouldn't we sit on the same side?"

Before Tori could reply, the man beside her said, "We're not squaring off for a fight, Miss O'Connor."

Unhappy, Kate couldn't think of a counterargument. Without looking at the man waiting patiently beside her, she slid into the booth across from the lawyers.

As soon as they were seated, Hardison's attorney opened his briefcase and efficiently withdrew a stack of papers. "Fortunately I brought an extra copy," he said with a smile directed to Tori.

Kate was surprised to see the sparks that flew between the two lawyers. Not that Tori wasn't worth a second look. Though she was dressed as the consummate professional, she would turn heads on any street corner.

The lawyer passed out the agreement. "Let's go through this together," he said and, after a quick look around, began explaining each paragraph. "The first paragraph is introductory and indicates this is a contract for services rendered, spelled out below, with compensation."

Madge arrived at the table with coffee for everyone and there was a break in the explanation while she served them.

Kate read ahead, anxious to get to the terms of the contract. Maybe Mr. Hardison had changed his mind, altered his requirements, made it impossible for her to accept. It would be painful to pull back from her dreams now.

She ignored the lawyer's voice as he returned to his explanation. Having found the paragraphs that outlined Hardison's requirements and "compensation," she eagerly read his terms.

Until she reached the clause about fidelity.

"You don't care if I have affairs?" she asked, interrupting.

He hadn't been following along, she realized, as he grabbed his paper off the table. "Where does it say that?"

"We discussed that part, Will, remember?" his lawyer said pointedly.

"I don't recall anything about *her* having affairs."

Chapter Four

Will took a deep breath, wondering what had come over him. He hadn't had such a bad case of foot-in-mouth disease since he was a boy. But the thought of Kate O'Connor in another man's bed had destroyed his sense of self-preservation.

"I didn't mean that the way it came out," he hurriedly said as Kate's lawyer opened her mouth.

"I hope not. Equality for women was established a long time ago," Tori said mildly.

"Exactly why that clause applies to either party," Charles said smoothly, smiling at the lady. "What my client meant to say is that we discussed his celibacy, but not Miss O'Connor's."

Will took a quick look at the beautiful woman beside him, but she seemed disinterested. When Charles asked if she had any problems with the clause, she shrugged her shoulders.

"This isn't a love match. I don't require devotion for a business agreement."

"Very realistic," Charles praised.

Will wasn't quite ready to voice his pleasure at being dismissed on a dollars-and-cents basis. She was right, of course. They were only discussing business. And as long as he didn't look at her, feel her sitting beside him, smell her elusive perfume, perhaps he could remember that.

"Shall we sign, then?" Charles asked, pulling a pen from his inner coat pocket and handing it to Will.

"Yes," Kate agreed, pulling out her own pen.

"Kate, I think we should take twenty-four hours, which would give me time to read the agreement more thoroughly," Tori advised, frowning slightly.

"I promise it's a straightforward agreement," Charles said, smiling at Tori.

"I'm sure it is but—"

"I don't want to wait," Kate said, writing her name. "Do I need to sign all the copies?"

"Yes, of course," Charles said.

She shoved her completed copy at Will and stared at him, waiting for him to put his name on the one in front of him. With a shrug, he complied. At least he wouldn't feel he'd forced her into anything.

When all the copies had been signed, Kate turned to him. "Do we have time to get the marriage certificate today?"

"Today?" Will questioned. "Why would we get it today? It's only good for a week or two after you get it."

For the first time he saw emotion in her hazel eyes.

But he wasn't sure if it was fear or sadness. And he couldn't figure out a reason for either.

"But we have to marry at once. I want to get started on the renovations."

"We're certainly not going to have some hole-in-the-wall wedding. Nothing could be worse. My mother would think that I'm embarrassed by my choice, and she'll believe it won't last."

Though she straightened her shoulders and lifted her chin, which only brought emphasis to her lovely figure, Kate said calmly, "But you *are* embarrassed by your choice, and we both know it won't last."

He ignored the second part of her claim, but the first couldn't pass undisputed. "You're wrong. You didn't embarrass me last night. I'm not a snob."

She looked away. "We need to be married at once."

So she wouldn't discuss last evening? He wanted her to look at him. "Did I make you think you embarrassed me?"

This time when she looked at him, her lips tilted on one side, a roguish grin starting. "No, I guess not. After all, *you* didn't pass out."

"Who passed out?" Tori demanded. "I haven't heard this story."

"Never mind," Will said, "it isn't important."

"I believe I could enlighten you over dinner," Charles suggested softly.

Tori appeared startled by Charles's offer, but Will wasn't. He'd already sensed his lawyer's interest in the other woman.

"Why don't we make it a foursome, celebrate the agreement?" Tori suggested.

Will knew Charles would be no more happy with that suggestion than he was, but neither of them said anything. Tori looked at Kate for an answer.

"Probably Mr. Hardison already has plans, Tori. And I really need to work." The idea of an intimate dinner—even with Tori and Charles as chaperones—suddenly made her uncomfortable. If she and Will Hardison were to have a platonic marriage, she'd prefer to avoid any cozy occasions. After all, she was human...and he was devastatingly attractive.

"Work where?" He wasn't aware she had a job.

"Here," she replied briefly. "When will the wedding take place? The timing affects my plans."

He frowned. She seemed fixated on a date. "I figure you and Mother can pull something together in a couple of months."

She appeared stunned, and he wondered if he'd upset her by rushing the wedding.

Instead she picked up one of the copies of the agreement and ripped it in two. "Then the deal is off."

Charles grabbed the other three copies for safekeeping, and Will seized Kate's hands. "What are you doing?"

"Destroying the agreement," she explained calmly.

"Kate, you signed them. I asked you to wait, but you said—" Tori began.

"Okay, so it's my fault, but I didn't think to specify the date for the wedding. I assumed he wanted results as fast as I did. But I can't last two more months.''

''What do you mean, you can't last?'' Will demanded.

''The diner is losing money every day. I don't have enough funds to keep it going.''

''Shut it down.''

She turned on him as if he'd wounded her and she needed to protect herself. ''Shut it down? Just like that? Destroy my dreams, my father's world?'' She shoved his shoulder. ''Get out of my way.''

Surprised by her sudden emotion, he slid from the booth, not sure what she intended. Without another word, she ran down the aisle of the diner and disappeared behind the kitchen door.

He collapsed on the bench seat and stared at his companions. ''What just happened?''

Charles shook his head, appearing as lost as Will.

Tori finally said, ''Kate wouldn't have made this agreement if she weren't desperate. She told me earlier that she was almost broke. If she didn't do something at once, she would lose the diner.''

Looking around him, Charles muttered, ''Small loss.''

Tori became almost as ferocious as Kate. ''That's a matter of opinion! This diner means everything to my client!''

''Sorry, Tori. I didn't mean to appear insensitive, but…well…I'm sorry.'' He looked at Will to help him out.

''Neither of us seemed to realize the difficulty, Tori. Look, I'm going to receive benefits immediately even though the marriage won't be for several months. I'm willing to give Kate the money at once.''

''But that's not what the agreement says,'' she reminded him.

''It doesn't matter. Kate and I will both honor the agreement,'' he said and then stopped, his mind spinning with that avowal of faith in a woman's word. What was wrong with him? He knew from experience a woman only did what helped her.

''Are you sure, Will?'' Charles asked. ''If you—''

''Kate will keep her word,'' Tori insisted.

''We could write an addendum, allowing the early payment. Would Kate sign that?'' Charles said, ignoring Tori's faith.

''Do whatever you have to do, Charles, but I'll have a check for Kate in the morning. Will you tell her, Tori?''

''Of course. And I know she'll agree to sign whatever is necessary. Thank you for being so understanding.'' She smiled as she motioned for Charles to let her out of the booth.

Before she could leave the table, Will added, ''And make dinner tonight a condition of the agreement.''

''Is that really necessary?'' Tori asked.

''Yeah, it is.''

Tori left the table, and Charles leaned across it. ''What are you up to?''

''I need to be seen in public with my fiancée. Otherwise, Mother won't believe the story. It's just part of the role I'm playing.''

''But do you have to horn in on my date? I'd like

to have the lovely Tori to myself,'' Charles complained.

"She seems almost as cautious as Kate. I don't think she'll accept your dinner invitation without Kate, so you probably owe me some gratitude instead of complaining.''

"I haven't needed your help getting a date since freshman year in college,'' Charles protested.

Will grinned. The two of them had been roommates in college, and Will had set his friend up on a blind date that had been a disaster. "Maybe things will work out better this time.''

Kate checked her appearance in the small mirror. At least she was dressed appropriately this evening. Her short black skirt, black hose and heels were brightened by a long-sleeved green silk blouse. She tied her red curls back with a green print scarf and lightly applied makeup.

In the morning. Her future husband had promised a check in the morning. If she'd remained reasonable, explained her difficulty, would the results have been the same?

She was lucky he hadn't grown disgusted with her temper and agreed to dissolve their agreement. *Sorry, Pop, I almost blew it.* Her father had warned her about losing her temper.

But now she could start the renovations at once.

Madge knocked on her door. "Your friend's here,'' she called.

Good. Tori had arrived before the two men. They'd all agreed to meet back here. Kate had even offered to cook for them, but Will Hardison had vetoed the idea, explaining that they needed to be seen in public to convince his mother of his sincerity.

It went without saying that the diner wasn't appropriate for that purpose.

But one day it would be.

With a quick spray of perfume, she grabbed her purse and walked through the swinging doors to the diner. Expecting Tori, she almost tripped when she was confronted by her future husband.

"Oh! I—I thought Madge meant Tori."

"You don't consider me a friend?" he asked, a smile on his lips.

Awkward question. "Perhaps in the future. We haven't known each other that long."

"True. Maybe tonight we can find out a little bit more about each other. I really do want us to be friends."

He reached out and took her hand in both of his, enveloping it in warm strength.

Surprised by the shortness of breath that struck her with his touch, she gave him a brief smile and tugged her hand away.

"You'll notice I let go of your hand at once. I don't want to have to go home to change clothes," he teased.

"A good idea, because spaghetti sauce doesn't come out as readily as champagne," she agreed, the corners of her lips lifting.

"Ah. That's what I smell. I think I might like to sample your cooking some time soon."

She was pleased with the compliment but refused to let him know it mattered. "If you're lucky."

Tori and Charles came in the door together.

"See, they haven't come to blows yet," Charles said.

"What are you talking about?" Will asked.

"Tori was worried that you two might have another fight before we could arrive to act as buffers."

"There's nothing to worry about. Kate and I were just discussing our future friendship," Will assured Charles.

Kate caught Tori's surprised look and offered her friend a smile in return. Kate could understand Tori's lack of faith in her agreeableness. She'd seen Kate lose her temper more than a few times. *But I'm going to stay calm for Pop's sake.*

"Shall we go?" Charles asked. "I'm starving."

Will insisted on driving, so Kate once again settled in the front seat of his Jaguar. She could get used to such luxury…which, considering her earning power at the moment, wasn't a good thing.

They went to Fedora's, a chic restaurant on the Plaza, the elegant shopping area in Kansas City. Kate wasn't surprised when Will's name gained them the privilege of being seated at once, though the restaurant was crowded.

As they walked to their table, the two men seemed to greet almost all the patrons.

"I think I may owe you," Tori whispered to Kate.

"Why?"

"It can't hurt my reputation to be seen with Charles

Wilson. He's already a partner in a very prestigious firm.''

''His father's firm. Are you sure he earned it?''

''Oh, yeah,'' Tori returned. ''I'm sure.''

''Ladies,'' Charles said, holding out a chair for Tori as Will did the same for Kate.

After they were seated, Kate concentrated all her attention on the menu, reading the description of each offering as if she were studying for a test.

''You must be starving,'' Will commented.

She stared at him blankly.

''Occupational hazard,'' Tori explained. ''Kate considers all restaurants her competitors.''

Kate offered her companion an apologetic smile. ''Sorry, Mr. Hardison, but I want your investment to pay off.''

''Don't you think we could be a little more informal, at this stage?'' he asked her. ''After all, we are engaged.''

''All right, sorry, William.''

''Will.''

She'd heard several people address him as Will, but she was still surprised that the head of a large corporation would choose to be addressed by a nickname.

When she said nothing, he leaned toward her. ''Goes well with Kate, don't you think?''

Tori chuckled. ''Especially when you think of *Taming of the Shrew*. It took a lot of *will* for Petruchio to overcome Kate's temper.''

Kate groaned. ''Please. I'm tired of those jokes.''

"Have you two known each other long?" Will asked.

"Only since kindergarten," Kate replied.

"Ah, I thought there was more than an attorney-client relationship in that comment." He looked at Charles. "Charles and I met as freshmen roommates."

The conversation continued, and as they explored each other's backgrounds Kate was surprised to find she was enjoying herself.

By the time dinner ended, Kate believed she and Will could actually become friends, as long as she ignored the attraction that rose in her every time he leaned close or touched her.

As they were debating the wisdom of ordering dessert, they were interrupted by a distinguished older gentleman.

"Will? How are you, my boy?" he asked in a booming voice.

Will rose to his feet at once. Benjamin Atwood had long been a friend of his father's. "Ben! How nice to see you. How are *you?*"

"Fine, fine. I can tell you're fine, too," Ben said, his gaze roving over Will's dinner companions. "Are you going to introduce me to these two lovely ladies?"

Will made the introductions, including Charles. However, when he said Kate's name, he noticed that Ben's reaction was a quick frown. Kate greeted the man charmingly, so it couldn't be her behavior that caused it.

"Mind if I steal Will away for just a minute?" asked Ben, his smile not as warm as it had been.

Will accompanied him to the lobby, wondering what had caused the change in his friend. "Everything okay, Ben?"

"You tell me. Is that the young lady who upset your mother last night?"

Will stiffened. "Yes, it is."

"Boy, you'd best be careful. That kind of woman will trap you into marriage before you know it."

Will was surprised at how quickly his temper rose...almost like Kate's. "What do you mean, 'that kind of woman'?"

"I've heard from more than one source that she didn't belong at the gala. I'm sure it was as embarrassing for her as it was for your mother. Ladies like her might be fun for a change, but you don't want to embroil yourself with one permanently."

"Too bad, Ben, because I already have. I'll bet you've already heard that I told Mother we are to be married." He'd never considered Ben a snob, but it appeared he was wrong.

"Damn it, Will, sleep with her if you must and get her out of your system. But don't marry her!"

"Why not? She's the prettiest woman in the room. You can't deny that. What's wrong with her?"

"She's a waitress, damn it! You told your mother so yourself."

"I lied. She owns a diner. She's a businesswoman. I laid it on too thick because I wanted to irritate Mother. But even if she were a waitress, that's no reason why I shouldn't marry her." Will squared his jaw, becoming more irritated as the conversation progressed.

"You have nothing in common. Your father would be horrified."

"Would he? My father should be pleased. I have no intention of marrying someone like my mother, because I don't want to be miserable the rest of my life like him!"

"What are you talking about? Your father loved your mother." Ben seemed taken aback by Will's words.

"Never mind, Ben. Tell Mother you tried. I make my own choices, and I choose Kate."

"I think you're doing this just to aggravate your mother, boy, but I'm telling you, this woman may take advantage of you. Trap you. It's happened before."

Will felt guilty that his motives were so easily suspected. That meant he'd have to be a better actor than he'd thought. "Any man who gets Kate in his bed won't be complaining, Ben. Trust me on that one."

Ben muttered something under his breath, persuading Will that his old friend believed that Will had already shared a bed with Kate.

The longing that suddenly consumed him sent panic through his veins. He might wish others to think Kate had caught him by her charms, but he wanted to be able to control his physical response to her.

He had to admit, however, that he hadn't enjoyed himself this much in quite a while. Kate had a quick wit and a musical laugh that brought a smile to his lips whenever he heard it.

Not to mention the sexual attraction he felt.

Better not to mention that, he warned himself. Not if he intended to keep his distance and remain unsusceptible to her magnetism.

When he returned to the table, the other three had decided on desserts. They placed their orders and then relaxed.

"Where are you two going to be married?" Charles asked lazily. "I'll need to get my tux pressed if it's going to be formal."

"It will be," Will assured his friend, a smile on his face.

At the same time, Kate said firmly, "It won't be."

Tori looked apprehensive, Charles curious.

Will turned to Kate. "What are you talking about? Of course it will be. We'll be married in church—"

"Absolutely not. We can't do that."

"Did you plan on going to City Hall and standing before a stranger?" he asked, his voice rising with incredulity.

"A formal wedding isn't necessary…and would cost a lot of money."

He'd told himself women had cash registers where their hearts should be, but since he'd met Kate, he'd thought maybe he was wrong. Until now.

"Do you ever think of anything but money?"

His growl must have been more offensive than he'd intended—Kate blanched, and even Charles protested.

"This is a business arrangement," she muttered, looking away.

"I didn't mean to be rude, Kate, but I think I can

stand the expense of the wedding without cutting into your loan.''

''The wedding is the bride's expense,'' she said quietly.

Surprised by her words, he suddenly realized the difficulty. According to Tori, Kate had no money.

''If I'm paying for the bride, I may as well pay for the wedding, too.'' He intended his words to reassure her. He even smiled slightly.

To his surprise, anger gleamed in her eyes before she turned away.

Chapter Five

Kate refused to look at Will, but her attorney took umbrage for her.

"I see no need to insult my client because she accepted your offer of marriage."

"I didn't mean it as an insult," Will hastened to say.

"My client only spoke the truth," Charles chimed in.

Kate spoke up. "You're absolutely right, Mr. Wilson." Without pause, she added, "I find I don't care for dessert after all. Can we go?"

Will studied her face, but there was no trace of anger in her expression now. "Kate, relax. I didn't mean anything by my comment."

"As we've all agreed, you only stated the truth. And I still don't care to have dessert."

"Fine," he snapped, annoyed by her stubbornness. He waved the waiter over and canceled the desserts.

"Don't bother taking them off the bill," Will told him as picked up the tab for dinner. "I apologize for the inconvenience."

They walked outdoors in silence, waiting for the valet to bring the car. Once he was behind the wheel, Will tried again. "Kate, part of the plan is to have a visible wedding. That will require some kind of show. I thought you understood that."

"Your agreement didn't spell out the details," Tori observed from the back seat, while Kate remained silent.

"I didn't think it necessary to be quite so specific," Charles protested. "Anyone with common sense would see—"

"Are *you* insulting my client now, also? Like client, like attorney?" she returned quickly.

"You're being ridiculous," Charles snapped. "*Your* client signed the agreement, which clearly states that she must provide a visible presence."

"Which could be interpreted as making occasional appearances at his side as his wife. It doesn't necessarily translate to a big church wedding!"

As the battle of words raged in the back seat, Will watched Kate out of the corner of his eye. What was she thinking? Since they'd left the restaurant, she'd made no further comment.

As he pulled into the diner's parking lot, Will reached out to cover her hands, which were tightly clasped in her lap. Startled, Kate stared at him before turning away again and pulling her hands free.

"Kate? Will you forgive me for being insensitive?"

"There's nothing to forgive. I apologize for any misunderstanding. I will comply with whatever you think is necessary."

Her calm words startled him. A reasoned, sedate response wasn't what he'd come to expect from her. But it bothered him that she didn't once look at him as she spoke.

"Are you—"

"Don't look a gift horse in the mouth," Charles warned from the back seat.

"Well, really!" Tori huffed as she reached for the door handle.

"Wait, Tori, I didn't mean to offend you, but your client—"

"Has been perfectly reasonable." She got out of the car and slammed the door behind her.

"You'll still send the check in the morning?" Kate asked, gazing steadily at Will.

Ah-ha! There was his answer. She'd had time to consider her behavior and feared it might interfere with the flow of money. Back to the cash register heart. He answered her question with an abrupt nod.

In dealing with his mother, he'd learned the only way to control her was through finances. It appeared his pseudofiancée was just like Mother in that respect.

With a quiet thanks for dinner, Kate slid from the car and disappeared into the diner after her attorney, before Will thought to escort her.

"Well, that certainly worked out well," Charles said, his voice laden with sarcasm.

"What did you expect?" Will asked bitterly. "We're dealing with women."

* * *

As she brushed her teeth the next morning, Kate patted herself on the back for her calm response last night. It wasn't often she managed to hold on to her temper. *You'd have been proud of me, Pop.*

It hadn't been easy. She hadn't liked feeling that she'd sold her soul to Will Hardison.

But what was done was done, and she'd do it again. She was determined to restore The Lucky Charm Diner to its former glory...and make Lucky Charm Catering a well-known and respected name in Kansas City.

And it wasn't just for her. Kate and Maggie had talked about how Pop would've wanted to provide for Susan, their newly discovered sister. Making a go of the diner would let Kate do that.

She dressed eagerly, anxious to set her dream in motion. First she had to make breakfast for the regulars, start several dishes for lunch, then change clothes and go to the bank as soon as Will's check arrived.

Shortly after nine o'clock, in the middle of preparing her special spaghetti sauce, Kate heard Paula call her name. "Yeah?" she said without looking up.

"You got company."

She hadn't expected Will to deliver the check himself, but the shiver that coursed through her told her that she didn't find his presence unwelcome. Scary thought.

Untying the apron, she smoothed back several untamed curls that had escaped the barrette holding back her hair and slipped through the swinging door.

Expecting Will's tall, masculine presence, Kate didn't notice his mother standing by the front door until Paula waved her hand in the dowager's direction. Kate sucked in a deep breath.

"Mrs. Hardison? Hello, welcome to The Lucky Charm."

Her lips pressed tightly together, Kate's guest appeared anything but charmed. "I would like a word with you, Miss O'Connor."

"Certainly. Come this way. Paula, bring us each a cup of coffee, please."

She led the way to the last booth in the corner, where she'd met with Will and their respective lawyers. By the time they were both seated, Paula had arrived with the coffee.

"Need some cream, honey?"

Mrs. Hardison looked up at the waitress, affronted. "No, thank you."

"Sorry," Kate offered softly after Paula walked away. "She's used to waiting on truckers."

"I'm not surprised," Mrs. Hardison returned, her voice stiff with outrage.

Well, she'd tried to be generous, but Kate could only tolerate so much condescension. "Feel free to take your business elsewhere, Mrs. Hardison."

"I have every intention of doing so after I speak to you, Miss O'Connor." Rather than continue their conversation, she opened her purse and took out a checkbook. Flourishing a Mont Blanc pen that cost more than most people's food bill for a month, she then looked at Kate. "How much?"

"I beg your pardon?" asked Kate, momentarily confused.

"How much to abandon your plan to marry my son?" The woman's glare never wavered.

"You're insulting me, Mrs. Hardison," Kate said evenly, praying she could control her temper.

"Nonsense. I don't believe this is a love match. I would've heard about William's activities if he'd flaunted you in public. He's doing this to irritate me...or you've cast a spell on him. Whatever the case, I want you to jilt him."

"I'm sorry, I can't."

"You mean you *won't*. Don't you realize a marriage to you will ruin him?"

Kate opened her mouth to tear a strip off the snobbish woman's hide, but then reconsidered, moved by the genuine anguish she heard in the older woman's tone. "I promise I won't do him any harm, Mrs. Hardison," she said mildly.

"Not do him harm? You'll ruin all my efforts on his behalf!"

"If your son doesn't think—"

"What does he know? I've slaved tirelessly to keep first my husband and now William at the highest level of society. I've smoothed his path, given him connections—and now he's going to marry *you?*"

Kate swallowed her anger. This woman really believed what she was saying. But before she could respond, Mrs. Hardison spoke again.

"I'm prepared to be generous. Will fifty thousand do?"

Slapping a hand over her mouth, Kate tried to pretend her choking was a cough. Maybe she could make a career out of not marrying socially acceptable men.

"Mrs. Hardison, I—"

"Mother, what are you doing here?" Will growled, suddenly appearing beside the booth.

Mrs. Hardison had obviously no notion her son might appear—of course she knew nothing of the check that he'd evidently decided to deliver personally. She paled. "Why aren't you at work?"

"Never mind me. What are you up to?"

Kate was upset by the harsh way he spoke to his own mother. "Your mother was kind enough to pay me a visit," she lied. "I think it was very thoughtful of her."

Both Hardisons looked at her as if she'd lost her mind. Maybe she had. Why was she protecting a woman who considered her a social inferior and a gold digger? Kate supposed she was touched by Mrs. Hardison's concern about her son.

"I thought I made myself clear!" Will's mother exclaimed.

Kate swallowed the chuckle that almost escaped her. Before she could say a word, Will gave a loud sigh.

"Exactly what does that mean? What did you say to Kate?" he challenged his mother.

Kate wondered at his vehemence. Was this part of his act, or did he feel obliged to protect her from his mother's insults?

"I offered her money to back out of the engagement," Mrs. Hardison admitted, surprising Kate by her honesty. "You've made a mistake, even if you don't recognize it yet."

"I haven't made a mistake. You're the one who's got it wrong. Kate is perfect for me, and we're going to be married," he insisted, his voice tightening. His eyes narrowed. "And I expect you to make her feel welcomed into the family."

Kate felt as if she were watching a tennis tournament...except *she* was the ball! Before Mrs. Hardison could defy her son's order, Kate slid from the booth. "I'm sure you two can carry on your argument without me. I have something on the stove in the kitchen."

Though she heard Will protest her departure, she ignored him and continued on to the kitchen. As she was strapping on her apron again, she saw Will push opened the kitchen door, his mother on his heels.

"Kate, I want to apologize on Mother's behalf," he said at once.

Kate looked at his stern features, then turned to Mrs. Hardison, whose expression was just as stubborn as her son's.

"Okay," Kate returned, her attention focusing on her spaghetti sauce. After stirring it, she lifted the wooden spoon and sipped the concoction. Hmm, a little more oregano.

"Are you listening?" Will demanded.

She looked over her shoulder. "Of course I am." She selected what she wanted and added a teaspoonful to the sauce, then stirred with a clean spoon. She left it to simmer a while and turned to the oven where she'd begun a roast an hour earlier.

"Are you the only cook the diner has?" Will suddenly asked.

Kate looked at him in surprise. "Yes."

"Oh!" Mrs. Hardison moaned. "He's marrying a short-order cook."

Kate ignored the woman's lament, poking the roast with a fork to check its tenderness. Its aroma permeated the air in the kitchen.

Closing the oven, she returned to the spaghetti sauce. She needed to check the seasoning again. Just as she lifted the spoon to her lips, a shriek from the diner startled everyone. Before they could move, the swinging door opened and a small animal ran through. The sauce from Kate's spoon flew into the air, then splattered against Mrs. Hardison's pink suit.

Paula was next through the door, followed by several regulars, retirees who took their morning coffee at the counter every morning.

"Where did he go?"

"What? What was that?" Kate asked, still staring at the red stains on Mrs. Hardison's suit.

"A dog! It got in when Billy came in for coffee. Just scooted past him before we could stop him," Paula explained. "Where did he go?"

To Kate's surprise, it was Will who pulled himself together enough to answer. "He went through that door."

Realizing he'd pointed to the door that led to her one-room apartment, Kate sighed. "Paula, see if you can help Mrs. Hardison get the spaghetti sauce off her suit. Is the dog violent, foaming at the mouth?"

Billy, a retired schoolteacher, chuckled. "No, Kate.

He's just a scared little puppy. Half-starved by the looks of it.''

Kate, always an easy touch when it came to the underdog, man or animal, hurried to her room. It wasn't until she was on her knees in front of the bed, that she realized Will had followed her.

''Is he there?''

Her head snapped up. ''I think so, but I'm going to need something to draw him out. Would you get a wiener out of the fridge for me?''

The morning hadn't gone as he'd planned.

Will had intended a quiet talk with Kate this morning, making sure she wasn't upset, then a ceremonial handing over of the check. Then he thought he'd offer lunch at one of the elegant restaurants on the Plaza.

Instead he was in the diner kitchen looking for a wiener for a stray dog while his mother was dabbing spaghetti sauce off her suit, and his fiancée was on her knees in her bedroom, peering under the bed.

He found what he was looking for and ignored his mother's pleas that he take her away from this madhouse. Instead he returned to the bedroom, pausing at the door to admire his fiancée's posterior clad in tight jeans.

She looked up, catching him staring, and he hoped she didn't notice the heat in his cheeks. ''Uh, I found one. Here.''

She took the wiener from him and broke off an end, then bent to hold her hand under the bed. ''Here, sweetie, come have a bite.''

Her voice was soothing, lilting, mesmerizing. Will

figured she could cast a spell with that voice. The puppy must have agreed because Will heard movement under the bed.

"That's right, baby, come on. I won't hurt you."

Will squatted down beside Kate and caught his first glimpse of the mutt under the bed. Obviously a mixed breed, the dog kept its brown eyes focused on the bits of meat still in Kate's hands.

While the dog concentrated on eating, Will reached out and caught it, quickly stroking it to reassure it of his friendliness. The poor thing was so starved, he scarcely noticed Will's touch.

"If you'll finish feeding it, I'll go warm a little milk. He'll need something to drink," Kate said, rising and leaving him alone with the dog before he could protest.

As the puppy gulped down the food, Will looked around the small room. His inventory didn't take long. The narrow bed, a television set, one old chair and a little table that also served as a nightstand, was all the furniture in the room.

Kate returned, carrying a cereal bowl, and sat down on the bed beside him. "I think he was starved," she said softly, watching the puppy chew.

"Yeah." He moved the dog so it could drink the milk. Like a child with a new treasure, the puppy began gulping the liquid so fast, Will feared he might drown himself.

"Ever done CPR on a dog?" he asked wryly.

Kate's rich laughter filled the room. "I hope it doesn't come to that."

"Me, too." He might not mind trying to resuscitate

Kate, however. His gaze focused on her full lips, wondering how they'd feel beneath his.

"Well, now, we have a problem."

Kate's words made him fear she'd read his mind. "What? What problem?"

"The puppy. What are we going to do with him?"

"Take him to the pound."

"Oh, no! We can't do that. They'll put him to sleep."

An uneasy feeling snuck into Will's stomach. It wasn't that he didn't like dogs. He did, but he'd never had one as a child and didn't have time for one now.

"You want to keep him?"

"I can't," Kate said with a sigh. "He can't stay in the diner. It's against health rules. And this is where I live."

"Yes. We need to talk about that."

She stared at him as if he'd mentioned martians. "I beg your pardon?"

"You need to find somewhere decent to live. I have the check with me, so you can find an apartment."

She continued to stare at him. "But why would I waste money on an apartment? I can stay here until we marry. Then I assume we'll live in the same house."

"Of course we will, but you can't continue to live here."

"Why not?"

He would have thought she was being intentionally difficult if he hadn't read the honest confusion in her hazel gaze. "Kate, you hardly have room to turn around. You certainly can't entertain guests here."

"I don't do a lot of entertaining, Mr. Hardison," she said, rising with the now-empty bowl, her voice filled with anger. "We need to—"

"Will? Are you in there?" Mrs. Hardison called.

"Damn," he muttered. "Yes, Mother, I'm in here. Wait a moment and—" He immediately realized he was surrounded by difficult women when his mother disregarded his words and pushed into the room.

"Is this a storage room? Why is there a bed?" she asked, looking from Kate to Will as if she suspected they'd spent the past few minutes engaging in frantic sex.

Kate lifted her chin, and Will's gaze traced her slender neck, wishing he could follow the same path with his lips.

"This is my apartment, Mrs. Hardison. As you can see, we've found the dog."

"Yes, nasty little thing. I'm sure it has all kinds of germs."

Will almost chuckled aloud as his mother took a step back, as if afraid of catching something. She was as receptive to the dog as she'd been to Kate.

"I've been told dogs are cleaner than humans," Kate said.

Hearing the battle lines being drawn, Will decided he'd best intervene. "I see you got the stains off your suit, Mother."

Distracted from the topic of the dog, Mrs. Hardison glared at Kate. "Not all of them. I'm sending you the cleaning bill, young lady."

"Certainly, though you had no business being in my kitchen," Kate reminded her.

She certainly gave as good as she got. He couldn't have picked a more perfect antidote to his mother, Will decided with a grin.

"Neither did that—that animal!"

"I know. And I have to get him out of here as soon as possible. Maybe Paula—I'll go see if Paula can take him."

Will remained seated on the bed, holding the dog, scarcely noticing when its little pink tongue licked his hand.

"William, put that animal down. I'm sure it's dangerous to hold it."

"I don't think so, Mother. He's more scared than you are."

"You must offer this young woman a proper settlement and get out of this entanglement. Surely now you can see how inappropriate she is. She can't possibly fit into our world."

"She fits just fine in mine, Mother."

Before she could protest his words, his mother had to move to one side as Kate returned.

"No one can take him. Will, could you—I know he looks bad now, but when he's cleaned up, he'd be company for you. Please? They'll put him to sleep!"

The anguish in her voice and eyes might have convinced him to accept the stray. He'd like to think he would have agreed. But once his mother spoke, he had no choice.

"I forbid such a thing. My son will not take a *mutt* into his household!"

"You're wrong, Mother. That's exactly what I'm going to do."

Chapter Six

Four hours and a hundred and fifty dollars later, Will had a dog.

He'd insisted he couldn't pick the dog up from the veterinarian's office unless Kate accompanied him. She agreed, though reluctantly it seemed to him, since the time would be after the lunch rush.

"Aren't you a handsome doggie!" Kate said as she petted the bundle of fur.

"I think you're getting carried away, Kate. I admit he's improved, but handsome?"

Kate covered the puppy's ears. "Hush, he might hear you!" Her accompanying grin made her almost irresistible.

Will shook his head in mock disgust. "I wish you were as concerned about my feelings as you are about the dog's."

She immediately frowned. "What are you talking about? I came with you."

"I know, but we need to talk about where you live." He hadn't forgotten their abbreviated conversation earlier.

Stiffening, she stared straight ahead. "I agreed to marry you, but it is a business decision. My personal life has nothing to do with you."

"Yes, it does."

"I should think my living arrangements would be perfect for your plans."

He frowned, wishing he hadn't revealed so much of his intentions when they'd made their agreement. "True, but I don't see any need for overkill."

"Fortunately it's not your decision."

"Kate, you're being unreasonable. You have enough money now to find a decent place to live."

"I have enough money to fulfill my dreams. I can't afford to waste it on self-indulgence," she said, then returned to her one-sided conversation with the dog, as if their discussion had ended.

He frowned as he thought about her words. His mother would never consider improving her living conditions as self-indulgence. In fact, she was insisting she needed to redo the entire house since its decor was already three years old.

"If you found a place to live, the dog could live with you." He thought he'd found a way to tempt her to his position as she frowned, studying the wriggling puppy in her lap.

Then she looked at him, a grin on her lips. "But he's going to live with you eventually, when I do, so he might as well get used to his home now." Suddenly she gasped. "You don't live with your mother, do you?"

He rolled his eyes. "Kate, I'm thirty-four years old. That's a little old to be living with Mommy, don't you think?"

She ignored his question. "In an apartment?"

"No, a house."

"With a fenced yard?"

"Yes, with a fenced yard. I'll even buy a doghouse, okay? Can we stop discussing the dog's living arrangements and get back to yours?"

"Nope. We have something much more important to discuss," she assured him, her eyes sparkling.

His gut clenched with unexpected desire. When she smiled that way, he'd promise her almost anything, he realized. He'd better be on his guard. "What do we have to discuss that's so important?"

"His name."

With all kinds of possibilities running through his head, it took a moment to realize what she meant. "*That's* what is important?"

"Yes. I can't keep calling him puppy. What do you think he should be named?"

"How about Mop? That's what he looks like."

"How cruel! I bet there's a Prince underneath all that hair."

"Or at least a Duke," Will agreed, sarcasm in his drawl.

"Good. That will be his name. See, Duke? Will really likes you. He gave you your name," she assured the puppy, stroking him lovingly.

Will said nothing as he pulled into his driveway.

He was more interested in what Kate thought about his home than the dog's name. Not that her opinion was really important. After all, it was a business agreement, as she frequently reminded him, but he waited for her reaction anyway.

After he stopped the car in the circular driveway, he turned to stare at her. She never noticed. Her eyes were wide as she looked at the two-story English manor-style house.

"You live here by yourself?" she finally asked quietly.

"I have a housekeeper."

She turned to look at him, frowning and chewing on her bottom lip. "I never realized how desperate you were."

"Desperate?"

"To get your mother to leave you alone."

"Why would my house make you think that?"

"You live in a palace. I live at the diner. There's a considerable difference in the two."

Everything she said was true, but it bothered him, somehow. "I don't think you need to sacrifice by continuing to live there for our agreement."

Her chin shot up and he realized he'd been insensitive again. "I don't consider living at the diner a sacrifice. I have everything I need and it's convenient. I think Duke needs to get out of the car."

Before he could say anything to make up for his ill-chosen words, she and the dog got out. As soon as she set the dog down on the manicured lawn, he proved her right.

Once he'd finished his business, he came right back

to Kate's feet without her having to call him. With adoring eyes, he pleaded for her to pick him up.

Will understood exactly how he felt.

The next few days were frantic for Kate. She hired an architect and showed him around the diner, explaining exactly what she wanted. She interviewed several builders and accepted estimates. And she pored over restaurant equipment brochures and calculated purchases well into the night.

In addition, she continued to do the cooking for the diner, relying on Madge and Paula to heat things up when she had to be away.

And once, she ventured to Will's house in her father's decrepit old car to visit Duke. It angered her that she allowed his magnificent house to intimidate her. But even that couldn't allow her to completely abandon Duke.

When she returned to the diner that afternoon in time to prepare dinner, Madge met her at the door.

"Your guy called. Wants you to call at once."

Her guy? Somehow she didn't think Will would appreciate that appellation. "Thanks, Madge." She entered the kitchen and picked up the phone, dialing Will's office number.

"Madge said you called," she said as soon as Will answered.

"Why didn't you tell me you were going to visit Duke?" he demanded.

Instantly she decided he didn't want her showing up at his house. Maybe the neighbors had complained. "I'm sorry. Next time I'll ask permission."

"Kate, I didn't mean—I wanted to see you. Since you've turned down every invitation I've extended this week, I thought you wouldn't object if *I* visited with *you* while *you* visited with the blasted dog!"

"I—I thought—never mind. I didn't think you'd have time during the day. Your housekeeper said Duke is doing quite well."

"Quite well? She must be afraid of hurting your feelings."

"Is he causing problems?" What would she do if Will wouldn't keep Duke?

After a silence that said more than she wanted to know, he sighed and said, "No, no, he's fine. But I demand equal time. If you can spare an afternoon for Duke, you can spare an evening for me."

Guilt filled her. After all, her agreement had said she would be visible. In fact, she'd scarcely seen him since Duke had interrupted his mother's visit.

"Well, I suppose I could spare one evening," she agreed.

"Don't make it sound like you're going to a hanging," he replied, exasperation in his voice.

"I'm sorry. But I need to make it a late dinner. Could you wait until nine?"

"Kate, I run a multimillion-dollar business. How can you be busier than me?"

Kate chuckled. "Perhaps you're a better executive than me. After all, you've had all that experience."

"Nine o'clock and not a minute later!" he snapped and hung up the phone.

Will knew he'd sounded testy on the phone. So he brought a dozen roses along when he arrived that night. He could apologize for testiness. It would be harder to apologize for…admit, even…the hunger to see Kate.

After all, they were talking about a business agreement.

He stepped into the diner and met Madge's stare. She nodded her head toward the kitchen.

Through the swinging doors, he discovered Kate stirring something on the stove, a large apron covering most of her.

"It's nine o'clock," he said as a greeting.

"I won't be but a minute. A customer wanted a special order—a California omelet. It won't take long."

Her cheeks were flushed from the heat of the stove and she didn't even look his way. Grabbing a plate from the stack on the shelf above her, she slipped the egg dish onto it, added a piece of parsley and a slice of orange and put it on the window shelf where Madge could get it.

Then she whipped off her apron and turned to face him. "I'm ready. Almost on time." She added a big smile that made him want to hold her.

He gave in to his wants and pulled her to him, his lips covering hers before she could protest. It was their first kiss. He hadn't planned for such a romantic moment to take place in the old kitchen, but then he hadn't really planned for a romantic moment.

Her lips were soft, inviting, luring him deeper and deeper, making him forget his surroundings. Her body pressed against his brought thoughts of bed, bare skin, blazing, all-consuming sex.

It was Kate who ended their embrace. She pushed her way out of his arms, her eyes wide, her lips trembling. "We—we need to go, don't we?"

His mind was so befuddled, he could scarcely think. Go where? To bed? He took a step toward her and she held out a hand to keep him away.

"Oh. Yeah, to the restaurant," he agreed, trying to pull himself together. A kiss had never disturbed him as much as that one had.

Without a word, Kate pushed through the swinging door to the main part of the diner, where they were surrounded by people. Or at least two or three people.

"We're going, Madge."

She was almost out the door before Will remembered the roses he'd laid on the cabinet when he'd taken Kate in his arms. "Madge, could you put the roses in a vase? Thanks."

Kate stepped outside and then looked at him. "You brought roses?"

"Yeah. I forgot them because—I forgot them." He opened the car door for her. A good thing he'd caught himself. It wouldn't do to let the woman know how much power she had over him with one kiss.

After joining her in the car, he explained their destination. "I thought we'd go to the Plaza again, but this time I've picked a quiet restaurant."

"All right."

He wanted to be able to have conversation this evening, to find out what was occupying her time. But they'd gotten off on the wrong foot. For a conversation, that is. But he wouldn't mind repeating that kiss. In fact, if he didn't stop thinking about holding her again, he wouldn't be able to get out of the car without embarrassing himself.

Once they were in the restaurant and seated at a table, he relaxed. Until he noticed a puzzled expression on Kate's face.

"What's wrong?"

"I thought the purpose of our going out was to be seen," she said, leaning toward him.

He fought to bring his gaze to her face, instead of the suddenly plunging neckline of her blouse as she bent down. "Uh, yeah, it is."

She looked around the restaurant and back at him. "The lighting is rather dim, and the restaurant is quiet. Do you think anyone will see us?"

Raising an eyebrow, he watched her carefully. "A lot of important people dine here. I'm sure we'll be seen."

No sooner were the words out of his mouth than Charles and Tori passed by their table.

It was Tori who saw them and asked if they could join their friends. It was Kate who immediately agreed. The two men exchanged rueful looks.

Charles slapped Will on the back and leaned down to whisper, "We're going to have to coordinate our movements better if we're ever going to get our ladies alone."

Will nodded as he stood and moved around the table to join Kate. At least he'd get to sit closer to her. But that was small compensation for losing their privacy.

Several hours later, he escorted Kate back to the car. Maybe their being joined by Charles and Tori wasn't such a bad thing after all. It took his mind off the desire that filled him whenever he looked at Kate.

Until now, of course. Once he joined her in the car, he leaned over and brushed her lips with his, taking her by surprise.

"Why did you do that? Was someone watching?" she asked as she pressed against the back of her seat.

"Uh, yeah, someone was watching." He repeated his action. When she turned her head away, he added, "It would look better if you'd cooperate a little."

She hesitated, then slid her arms up his chest to link behind his neck. With a sweetness that almost destroyed what little control he had, she turned her lips to his. He met her more than halfway, drawing her against him, his lips molding hers.

Sometime later, she pushed against his shoulder and twisted her lips from his. "Will, we can't—that's enough. Half of Kansas City must've seen us by now."

"Uh, right. I'll—I'll start the car."

He put the car in motion, working hard to concentrate on the traffic rather than the woman beside him.

Hungry to touch her again, he considered various options to extend the evening. "Uh, want to visit with Duke?"

Her eyes rounded in surprise. "At this hour? Won't he be asleep?"

"He'd probably wake up for you." He let his gaze stray from the road to focus on her slightly swollen lips.

"I think it's too late. I have to be up early in the morning." She didn't look at him.

With a sigh, he gave up. When he parked at the diner, however, he hurried to her side of the car.

"You didn't need to get out, Will. I could—"

She never got to finish her sentence because Will's lips had returned to hers, with a hunger borne of their earlier tasting. To his pleasure, she didn't resist, or pretend disinterest. Her arms slid around his neck and she opened to him at once. As if she wanted him, too.

Until one of the patrons leaving The Lucky Charm Diner called out to them. Kate ripped herself from his embrace and raced into the diner.

Kate slammed pots and pans with abandon the next morning. She needed to release her frustration...and fear. William Hardison was proving to be a problem. A sexy, confusing problem.

She wanted to concentrate on the diner, its operation, its improvement, its future. *Her* future counted on it. And that of Maggie and Susan and her family. But instead, her thoughts continued to turn to Will and those moments in his arms.

"Damn!" she cried as she burned her finger on a hot pan. That was careless, and all Will's fault, she insisted to herself as she ran cold water over her burn.

Paula's head appeared in the opening. "You okay in there?"

"Yeah, I'm fine." She dished up the omelet she'd been preparing.

"How about—oops! You've got company again."

She could tell by Paula's tone of voice that she

wasn't going to like the identity of her visitor. Her mind immediately flashed a picture of Will.

"Hello?" a soprano voice called out, immediately identifying the caller.

"It's that society lady, the one with the spaghetti stains," Paula added, which left no doubt.

With a sigh, Kate pushed back stray curls, wiped her hands on the apron and pushed open the swinging door to the diner. "Hello, Mrs. Hardison."

The woman nodded but showed no warmth.

Kate waited, saying nothing else.

"I assume you are still engaged to my son?"

"I assume so, unless you've heard something since last night," Kate replied, a small smile on her lips. After all, her recent parting with Will hadn't indicated an end to their agreement.

Mrs. Hardison didn't smile back. "Then we need to agree on a date for the engagement party."

Kate thought her knees were going to fold. Taking a deep breath, she stared at the woman. "An engagement party?"

"Yes. We should have it soon since William indicated he didn't want a long engagement."

"But I thought you—"

"Don't misunderstand me, young lady. I'm as opposed to this marriage as I ever was, but I know what is due for my son's engagement. Now, how do you feel about two weeks from tomorrow?"

Kate's head spun and she looked for an escape. "I think you'd best discuss this idea with Will."

The woman's eyebrows shot up. "I thought you would be thrilled with the idea. After all, I'm sure you're marrying him so you can be a part of society here in Kansas City.''

Kate felt her back stiffen and made an effort to relax. Gently she said, ''Mrs. Hardison, I want to cater for society, not be a member of it.''

''Cater? You mean cook? You want to *cook?* My dear, you can't cook for society once you marry William. You will be one of the leaders!''

Kate shook her head, a smile on her lips. The woman certainly had shifted directions. ''Really, I don't—''

''Now,'' Mrs. Hardison began, as if Kate hadn't spoken. ''We must make plans. You'll need to find an appropriate gown, of course. But with me to guide you, I'm sure we can find one in the next two weeks. You can give me a list of any guests you want to invite.'' She paused, then added, ''I don't want to offend you, my dear, but please be selective about whom you include.''

Kate's mind was on another track. She didn't have time to be offended. Was this the perfect opportunity? And could she pull it off without the proper equipment and staff?

''I'll agree to the party if you let me cater it.'' She held her breath, waiting for the woman's reaction.

''Don't be absurd! We're talking a guest list of at least two hundred people.''

Kate rattled off her credentials, more comprehensively than she'd given Will. Enjoying the astonishment Mrs. Hardison expressed, she clasped her hands in front of her and waited.

Though it was clear from her glare that Mrs. Hardison was unhappy with Kate's request, she nodded. "Very well. I'll accept your offer, but don't think to charge me outrageous prices. I certainly won't pay more than fifty dollars a person."

Kate blinked. "Are you serving a meal?"

"Of course not. Hors d'oeuvres. You do know how to make them, don't you?"

At fifty dollars a person, Kate figured she could make all the hors d'oeuvres out of caviar, if she wanted. Someone had been soaking Mrs. Hardison big time. "Yes, I do, and the bill won't be that much."

"I don't want anything skimpy."

Kate might accept criticism of her appearance, but not her cooking skills. She immediately suggested a comprehensive menu that left her future mother-in-law slack-jawed.

Chapter Seven

Kate had assumed convincing Mrs. Hardison of her abilities would be the hard part. She quickly discovered differently when Will took them to lunch that afternoon.

"Absolutely not!" Will stared at the two women facing him, wondering if they'd taken leave of their senses.

"I don't see why you would object, if your mother doesn't. I promise I'm capable of making excellent hors d'oeuvres," Kate returned, her hackles visibly rising.

"It's not a question of your competence, Kate. Though I think you are overestimating your ability without the proper equipment. It won't be installed by then, will it?"

He could tell he'd scored a point as her determined glare weakened.

"No, probably not. But it's such an excellent opportunity to show my abilities to the upper crust in Kansas City.''

''You'll have plenty of time for that. But I don't want you working during our engagement party. Besides, we're not going to wait two weeks.''

''We're not?'' Miriam Hardison screeched, sitting up straighter. ''But we certainly can't have it any sooner. I want—''

''It doesn't matter what you want, Mother. We'll have it at my house next Friday, a week from tomorrow, and the wedding four weeks later.'' He figured that would be enough time to pull something together. And then, after the wedding, he would have peace.

At least, that's what he thought until he looked at Kate. Peace from his mother, but would he have any peace from the hunger that filled him every time he saw Kate?

Miriam's lips moved, but no sound came out. Kate picked up the glass of water the waiter had left in front of her and handed it to Will's mother.

''Drink, please, Mrs. Hardison.''

After several sips of water, his mother set the glass down and patted Kate's arm. ''Thank you, dear. I only wish my son were as thoughtful. William, you can't possibly mean what you've just said. We cannot organize a wedding in four weeks.''

''Sure we can.''

''But the church. You won't be able to find a church available at such short notice. And a caterer. No, dear,'' she added as Kate opened her mouth, ''don't offer again. You cannot work at your own wedding.''

"Quite right, Mother. But we'll marry in my backyard, at two in the afternoon. If the minister isn't available, we know several judges who can perform the ceremony. All that's left is the florist, the caterer and the music."

Kate stared at him. "You sound as if you've planned a wedding before."

"No, but it's just a matter of organization. You can arrange for—"

"Me?" Kate demanded. "I'm getting the diner organized, redone. I won't have time to plan a wedding."

"Well, I certainly don't, with my new acquisition." He turned to his mother. "Well, Mother, you always wanted me to marry. Are you willing to plan the wedding?"

Miriam turned to look at each of them, a confused expression on her face. "You intend to marry at once but neither of you wants to plan it? Why don't you postpone it?"

He immediately erased the hope in his mother's gaze. "Nope, there will be no postponement."

The waiter interrupted their discussion to deliver their order. Will hadn't intended a long lunch today, but when his mother had called to confirm her plans, he'd immediately decided he needed to sit in on the discussion and had offered lunch.

When the waiter withdrew, Miriam, after a heavy sigh to show how put-upon she was, agreed to manage the engagement party and the wedding. "Though, of course, you're expecting me to work miracles."

The rest of the meal involved her questioning their

wants and tastes. Kate seldom expressed a preference, so Will made most of the decisions.

After eating, his mother hurried away, filled with numerous chores she had to perform. Kate rose, seemingly eager to return to the diner.

After they got into his car, he asked, "What will you wear to the engagement party?"

She seemed surprised by his interest. "My black dress. I told you that's as dressy as I come."

He remembered the black dress. It had made his mouth go dry then, and the memory of it had the same effect. But it wouldn't do. "You'll need to buy a long gown."

"No," she said, casually, as if it were a matter of taste.

"Yes. The engagement party will be formal. That's how Mother operates."

He pulled into the diner and parked the car. She opened her door, but turned to face him before getting out. "Remember why you wanted this agreement? If I'm dressed inappropriately, everyone will be happy."

He frowned. "But you would be unhappy."

"What does that matter?"

"It matters to me. I want you to wear an appropriate gown."

"Will, I'm not going to spend several thousand on a dress that I will only wear once when I could put that money to good use here." After saying her piece, she got out of the car and headed for the diner, as if their discussion was over.

"Wait!" When she ignored his order, he hurried

after her, catching her by the arm at the door. "Kate, you're not thinking. You can't—"

"Yes, I can. In fact, according to our agreement, that's exactly what I should do."

She stared up at him, her hazel eyes snapping with some emotion he couldn't read, her soft lips pursed in a stubborn line.

He fought the urge to pull her against him and kiss the stubbornness away. "I don't want you embarrassed."

"I can't afford it," she reiterated.

"I'll pay for a dress."

She opened her mouth to protest, and he couldn't resist. Wrapping his arms around her, he kissed her, her mouth already open to him. Kissed her until he forgot where they were, what he was supposed to be doing, or even that their engagement was a pretense.

He wanted her.

She pulled back, her hands leaving his shoulders to push against his chest. "No, Will, we mustn't— you're doing that too much."

"We have to look like this is a real marriage."

She blinked several times. "I'm beginning to worry about what happens after the wedding."

So was he. "I signed the agreement."

She licked her lips and he almost melted at her feet. "So did I, but—but there's a chemical reaction, or something, when we kiss each other, that makes everything go haywire."

"Yeah," he agreed, still holding her. His rioting hormones made any conversation difficult.

"I—I have to go."

"We haven't decided about the dress," he reminded her. Anything to keep her with him a little longer.

"Will, you're not listening."

"I told you I would pay for the gown."

"And then there's shoes, and—and undergarments, and a bag, and the list goes on. I can't let you pay for everything."

"Think of it as a uniform. I'll pick you up tomorrow after the lunch rush. We'll have you back before the dinner rush." He was learning how her schedule worked.

"But you need to work."

"I'm the boss. I can take off if I want." Of course, he'd have to reschedule a telephone conference with people in New York. And work late tonight to get everything done.

"Are you sure—I can take the money out of my budget."

He knew her offer was generous by the disheartened tones of her voice. "I'll be here at two. Be ready." He gave her one more quick kiss before she could protest, then he hurried back to his car.

Before he dragged her to that little bed in the room behind the kitchen.

Kate didn't know what Will was thinking. She'd understood his reasoning behind their agreement. But he was going against what she'd thought he'd do.

In fact, she couldn't even see a reason for the engagement party. It would only demand more time from his work.

But in spite of her confusion, she was ready when he picked her up the next day. "Are you sure you want to do this? I'll understand if you've changed your mind," she assured him.

"I haven't changed my mind. I have a list of places to shop from Mother." He smiled at her. "Much to my surprise, she was disappointed not to be included in the shopping trip."

Kate, too, was surprised. "I thought she wanted nothing to do with me. The engagement party was a surprise, too."

"It's the proper thing to do," he told her in mock hauteur.

"I think you're too hard on your mother."

"That's because she hasn't been trying to marry you off for the past ten years."

He snagged a parking place near an exclusive store on the Plaza. "She says this shop is the best, so we'll start here. And, Kate, no looking at the price tag. This is my treat."

Will expected to spend the rest of the afternoon, dragging after Kate from one store to another. However, after selecting four dresses in the first shop, she showed him only one, a dress that clung lovingly to her curves before flaring out slightly at the hipline.

Its royal blue color, with sparkling highlights like a night sky filled with stars, flattered her red hair and made her eyes look turquoise.

It was a simple style that suited her.

"Do you like this one?" she asked.

"What's not to like? You look beautiful."

The saleslady fluttered around them. "I think you should show him the pink one. It's more detailed. And made by a famous designer."

Will could translate those phrases to read a higher price tag. And more commission. He looked at Kate to discover her reaction.

"No, thank you. Since my fiancé likes this one, I believe this gown is the one we want."

"Very well," the woman agreed stiffly. "Will you need the accessories I brought you?"

"Yes, thank you."

"But Kate," Will began, "did she have everything you need? That was a long list you mentioned."

She shook her head. "She brought in everything I need." She raised the hem of the dress to show him blue shoes.

After he nodded, she slipped back into the dressing room, and he stepped up to the cash register, surreptitiously checking his watch. Half an hour. He'd never known his mother to select a pair of shoes in anything under three hours. Much less everything for an important party.

When they arrived back at the diner, he was reluctant to let her go. "We should've looked at rings."

"Rings?"

"Your engagement ring. We'll need to find one before the party."

"I don't think we should get one," she said as she gathered her purchases.

"What are you talking about? Of course you'll have an engagement ring."

"Will, I don't think you planned well. This agreement is costing you a lot more than you thought. Surely we can cut down on the extras.''

He stared at her. ''You consider an engagement ring an extra?''

''We're not having a real marriage so why—that's it. You can buy a cubic zirconia. No one will ever know.''

Will stared at her in surprise. He already knew she wasn't exactly like the other women he'd known, including his mother, but he was surprised by her words. It blew his theory that every woman was out for what she could get.

''I'll, uh, see what I can find.'' She couldn't really believe he would give her a cubic zirconia, could she? But she nodded, pleased that he'd agreed.

She gave him her ring size, thanked him for the dress and accessories and hurried back into the diner.

Leaving him time to return to the office. Why not? He had nothing else to do with himself. Of course, he could go home and play with Duke. The little dog was worming his way into Will's heart, in spite of his intentions to keep him at a distance.

Pretty sad when a man's best companion was a dog.

The next morning Will returned to the Plaza. He'd decided he should find an engagement ring himself, without consulting Kate. The way she was going, she might suggest buying a box of Cracker Jacks in the hope of finding a suitable ring as the prize. Several hours later, he came to the diner, feeling smug about the diamond in his pocket.

Paula, the morning waitress, was behind the counter, pouring cups of coffee. Will slid onto a stool and she automatically filled a cup for him.

"Hi. You looking for Kate?"

"Yeah, but I don't mind the coffee first. She's here, isn't she?" He picked up his cup and took a sip. Mmm, good coffee.

"Yeah, she's out back, working."

"Out back?" Will asked, still thinking about the excellent coffee. His coffee at home didn't taste this good. He'd have to ask Kate to show his housekeeper how to make it.

"Yeah, the workers came to tear out the back of the diner. I think we're going to have to shut down a few days."

"So she's directing them?"

Paula gave him a careful smile and a nod.

He took one more sip and stood. "Save that for me. I'll find her and be back."

He went through the kitchen to the back, hearing a lot of noise as he reached the door. He stepped outside and saw several men with sledgehammers. Along an area where they had obviously earlier plied their trade, he found Kate.

She was dressed in jeans and a T-shirt, wearing leather gloves, and pulling away a layer of metal from the side of the diner.

"Kate! What the hell are you doing?"

She gasped and stepped back. "Working. What do you think?" She grabbed hold of the metal and began pulling again.

"You'll hurt yourself. Stop that!" he ordered, striding to her side.

Glaring at him, she continued to tug, her muscles straining. "Don't bother me," she said, panting slightly.

Another man strode around from the back of the diner and Will called him over. "You, come take this from her."

The man nodded and came over, but Kate wasn't as willing to accept Will's order. As the man took hold of the metal, shifting her away, she turned to Will, anger radiating from her.

"What do you think you're doing?"

"Trying to keep you from hurting yourself. You're too delicate to do this kind of work."

"I am not. It will save money if I help them. We'll finish faster." She turned back to work again, as if her explanation made everything all right.

"Kate, you have enough money to do the renovation without working out here yourself. Come inside."

"Yes, but we need to make this transition quickly. My bedroom and the storeroom will be open and I don't want—"

"Your bedroom? Then you can't stay there."

She put her hands on her hips and glared at him. "Thank you, but I'm not an idiot! I'm going to stay at my sister's for a couple of days."

"I didn't even know you had a sister. Where does she live?"

"She has an apartment in North Kansas City. And

I actually have two sisters.'' Again she reached for the metal.

He caught her arm. "Why didn't you stay there to start with?"

Sighing, she turned back. "Because it's forty-five minutes away and tiny. But I'll manage for a couple of days."

Will felt as if he'd been run over. Kate seemed too busy to realize she was throwing a lot at him at once. In particular, he didn't want her forty-five minutes away.

Only because it would take more time to carry out his plan, of course. It had nothing to do with wanting to see her a lot more often than she seemed interested in.

"I think you should rent an apartment near here. There's some—"

She'd already returned to work. "Don't be silly, Will. That would be a wasted expense." She yanked the metal siding and then gasped as it gave way and she almost lost her balance.

"Kate, stop that before you get hurt. Hire another worker, if you must, but don't—"

She stepped back to face him. "Do I tell you how to do your job?"

He blinked. What was she talking about? Of course she didn't tell him how to do his job. "No."

"Then don't tell me how to do mine."

Will caught the grins of the men nearby. One of the men said, "That little lady is a pistol, ain't she?"

He could only agree.

"What is going on out here?"

Everyone turned to stare at Will's mother as she trudged around the back of the diner. She was dressed in a suit and heels, her fingers covered with rings.

Kate urged the men back to work, barely acknowledging Miriam's arrival.

"What is that child doing? It looks like she's working with these men. Explain, William."

Will looked from his mother to Kate and back again. "I can't explain it, Mother. Kate said something about needing to hurry the work along. I've been trying to get her to explain to *me,* but she's not much interested in conversation this morning."

He crossed his arms over his chest and waited.

"Kate!" Miriam shrieked.

"In a moment, Mrs. Hardison. I have to help carry this sheet of siding over to the other side." She continued on her way, leaving Miriam to stare in surprise.

"William, you cannot marry this woman. She ignores all polite behavior. She's working like a common laborer. And she's dressed like them, too!"

"I don't think she'd get a lot done dressed like you, Mother. I don't like her doing this kind of work, but you'll have to admit it's enterprising of her." He found a grudging admiration filling him. She was willing to work for her dreams.

"Make her stop," Miriam ordered.

Kate came striding back around the building.

"Kate," Will called, "Mother would like to speak with you."

With an exasperated look, Kate came over. "Yes?"

"Young lady, this is totally unacceptable."

Kate looked around her and then faced Miriam again. "What is unacceptable?"

"Your acting as a common laborer."

Kate rolled her eyes and looked at Will. "Tell her politely to mind her own business."

"It *is* my business. I'm here to take you shopping for a wedding gown," Miriam insisted before Will could speak.

Kate shook her head. "You should've called. I don't have time to shop for a wedding dress. I'll just wear a suit."

Miriam shrieked. "What? You can't! It's going to be a formal wedding! You must wear a long gown."

"Okay, I'll wear what we bought yesterday," Kate offered, already turning around to rejoin the workers.

"Is it white?"

Kate gave an exasperated sigh and faced them again. "No, it's blue. Now, could you both leave so I can get some work done? I don't want to impose on my sister any longer than I have to."

Will decided it was time to take charge. "You're not going to impose on her at all."

"Are you making all my decisions for me now?" Her hands went to her hips as she challenged him.

"I believe so. You see, you're going to move in with me, instead of your sister. It's a lot closer and it's where you're going to live anyway. We'll just be anticipating our vows by four weeks."

He smiled as both ladies stared at him in shock.

Chapter Eight

"What are you thinking?" Miriam shouted, stopping the workers in their tracks. "Do you want to be shunned by everyone who's important?"

Kate's gaze flashed to her pseudofiancé, seeing the spark of laughter that filled him, rendering him incredibly sexy. He turned to her and she had to strain to keep a straight face. Laughter ran through her as he invited her to enjoy his moment of success.

"Of course not, Mother," Will lied smoothly, "but I can't abandon Kate. After all, she's the love of my life."

In two strides he reached Kate and pulled her against him, whispering, "You can't refuse me now."

"William, you're being unreasonable," his mother protested. "I'll find room for Miss O'Connor in my house. That will keep everything proper."

"Kate would prefer to live with me. Wouldn't you, Kate?" Will asked, a determined glint in his eyes.

Kate shared the amusement with Will before saying politely, ''I believe I would, Mrs. Hardison, but I appreciate the offer. Will's house is—is closer to the diner.'' Her breath caught at the thought of moving into that lovely home, that much closer to Will. But it was part of her agreement. Wasn't it?

''Then it's settled. Let's go pack your things.'' He started pulling her toward the diner.

''But, Will, it will only be for a couple of days. So I won't have to pack much,'' she protested, resisting him.

''Nope. There's no point in your moving back here, only to move again in a few weeks. You might as well settle in for the duration.'' His charming smile almost erased the reminder that their agreement wasn't permanent.

Not that his mother realized his meaning, but Kate did.

''William, please, you're going to ruin our reputation,'' Mrs. Hardison pleaded.

''Mother, surely you don't believe every bride who wears a white gown is a virgin? Many people, even in the upper crust, cohabit before marriage these days.''

''But they don't thumb their noses at society rules. They sneak around,'' Mrs. Hardison said with an approving nod.

''And you think that's good?'' Will demanded. ''This is not Victorian England, Mother. I choose not to be so hypocritical. Come on, Kate.'' Again he tugged on her arm.

''Will, I'm working, remember?''

"No, you must come choose a wedding gown," Miriam insisted.

"Pack first, then the wedding gown," Will amended.

"No, I—"

"Lady," the foreman roared. "I don't care what you do, but make a decision. We're wasting time."

Kate looked around and realized for the first time that all the workers were watching the show going on before them rather than working.

Will leaned toward her. "They'll get more done with you out of here."

She was afraid he was right.

"All right," she agreed with a sigh.

"Good," Miriam agreed. "We'll start at Hall's. I've heard they have a good selection of off-the-rack gowns. That's probably the only way we'll find one in time for the wedding."

"I can't go like this," Kate protested.

"Absolutely not!" Miriam agreed, a horrified look on her face.

Will chuckled, and Kate feared he wanted her to embarrass his mother. Instead he said, "How about if Kate meets you at Hall's at three o'clock. She can shower, have lunch with me and do some packing and still make that, can't you, Kate?"

"So nice of you to ask me, since you're arranging my life," she said pointedly, her frustration showing.

"They close at six. That would only give us three hours," Miriam complained.

Before Kate could assure his mother she wouldn't need more time than that, Will spoke again. "Having gone shopping with my fiancée, Mother, I can assure you three hours will be more than enough time. In fact, I'll predict that you'll have time left over.''

"Don't be ridiculous, William. Shopping is hard work. We will have only begun at six o'clock,'' Miriam asserted.

Kate didn't want the woman's feelings hurt, even if Will was right. "But at least we will have started. I'm sorry I can't go right away, but I promise to be there at three o'clock.''

"Oh, very well. But I wish you would reconsider coming to stay with me until the wedding.''

"Absolutely not, Mother," Will answered for her. "I'm keeping her close to me. Society can snub us, if they want.''

With a sigh, his mother left.

"You shouldn't have looked so gleeful at the prospect of being snubbed. Your mother is going to get suspicious,'' Kate warned.

"Then we'd better convince her.'' He pulled her against him and lowered his lips to hers.

Kate's assumption that his mother was watching made it easy to justify her behavior. She slid her arms up his chest and around his neck, her fingers sliding through his silky black hair, her body pressed against his. The rush of excitement that flooded her transported her from the work site to a heavenly place.

When his hands slid beneath her T-shirt, however, she gasped and pulled back, remembering just in time that they had an audience.

"Will!''

"Sorry, I got carried away. Let's go inside," he murmured.

But Kate knew better than to be alone with him. With nothing and no one to interrupt them, to remind her of reality. "Um, I have to shower. You go have a cup of coffee and…and a piece of pie or something."

"If I'm going to substitute pastry for sex for the next year, I'm going to blow up like a balloon," he protested softly, so no one else could hear his words.

"I'll start making low-fat cakes and pies," she offered, a teasing smile on her lips.

"I think I prefer fat-free kisses." He moved toward her again.

Kate beat a rapid retreat, escaping into the diner as he followed.

"Okay, folks, the show's over. Let's get to work," the foreman hollered and the men obeyed, but their gazes lingered momentarily on the door where the romantic duo had disappeared.

Will slid onto the stool he'd previously occupied and Paula immediately filled another cup of coffee for him.

"You found her?"

"Hmm? Oh, yeah, I found her. She's showering right now."

"I'm glad you stopped her working out there. I was afraid she'd hurt herself, but she's so stubborn, I couldn't convince her."

Will grinned at the waitress. "I know what you

mean, but I had help. My mother arrived on the scene.''

Paula kept up a steady stream of chatter both with him and other patrons, and Will felt himself relax. When Kate appeared, however, his body revved up again, and he couldn't resist reaching out to touch her as she sat beside him.

"No pie?"

"Nope. I'm saving my appetite for something else.''

Her heated cheeks only increased his hunger.

"I think I'd better feed you.'' She slipped off the stool before he realized it and headed for the kitchen.

"Wait. I'll take you out to lunch.''

"Are you saying my cooking isn't good enough for you?'' she challenged from the swinging door.

"No, of course not. In fact, if that's roast beef that I smell, I suspect it will be the best I've ever had. But I didn't want you to have to work.'' In fact, he wanted to keep her close to him.

"It's already cooked. I put it on earlier. Two roast beef specials, coming up.'' She disappeared from view.

Again Will was reminded of the difference between Kate and the women he'd known in the past. They all expected to be waited on, seldom rose before noon and always had to be the center of attention.

Kate never stopped moving. She wanted to do everything for herself, and she resisted his help unless she found a way to pay him back.

In almost no time, Kate slipped from the kitchen and led Will to the back booth. Paula followed with two heaping plates of pot roast and vegetables, accompanied by a plate of flaky biscuits that melted in the mouth.

After the first bite, Will forgot about everything but satisfying his hunger. When he put the last bite into his mouth, he looked up to discover Kate smiling at him.

"I gather you liked it?"

"Liked? That's a mild term for the best meal I've ever eaten. You're an incredible cook."

"Thank you, kind sir. Now do you feel better about my chances to make a go of the diner and the catering firm?"

Her hopeful expression melted any reserve he might have had. "You've certainly got the cooking skills. How about the business sense to make a profit?"

She grimaced. "I don't know. Practicality is Maggie's talent, not mine. But I'm going to get her to help me."

"Maggie's your sister? What does she do?"

"She's an accountant with a big firm downtown."

"An accountant?" He couldn't imagine anyone related to Kate being staid and practical.

She grinned. "We're not at all alike. Maggie's quiet, conservative. Has no temper. Pop always said she was a changeling."

"Didn't you say you had a second sister?"

He didn't understand the almost confused look on Kate's face.

"Yes, but we didn't know about her until Pop's death."

"Are you sure she's your sister? Maybe she just hoped to cash in on an inheritance."

Kate laughed, a full, rich sound that entranced him all the more. "This is the inheritance, Will," she said, gesturing to the diner. "Would you go to all that trouble for this?"

His lips twitched with humor. "Probably not."

Kate smiled back at him and then sobered. "I remember Susan's mother, because I was four when Pop married her. But the marriage ended after about six months. Pop didn't know Sally was pregnant when she left. He never heard from her again."

"Then how—"

"He read about her death apparently, about a year ago. It was a small notice in the paper, but when he saw that she was survived by three children, he decided to check up on them." Kate paused to sip her tea. "He hired a private detective."

Will raised his eyebrows in surprise. Most men wouldn't have bothered.

"Pop worried about her for a long time after she left," Kate said, as if in explanation. "Anyway, shortly before his death, the detective brought him proof that Susan was his child. He changed his will, but he never contacted her."

Will reached out to clasp Kate's hand, hoping to ease the worry on her face. He recognized a sudden urge to make everything smooth for her.

"Maybe he was concerned about how she would react."

"I guess so. Pop—Pop was special. He tried to take

care of the world. I suspect he felt guilty that he hadn't known about Susan. But it wasn't his fault!''

''Of course not,'' Will assured her. He was discovering Kate was fiercely loyal as well as generous. ''What's Susan like?''

That bright smile he was coming to love spread across Kate's face. ''A lot like Pop. She's determined, loyal, loving. When her mother died, Susan's half sister was seventeen, and her half brother was seven. Susan has taken on the responsibility of raising them.''

''That's quite a load.''

Kate leaned forward. ''That's one reason it's so important that I succeed. Susan and Maggie both own a third of the diner. If we make money, it will help Susan.''

''Not Maggie?''

Smiling again, Kate said, ''Maggie has a big savings account. She tried to give it to me for the diner, but she's not really enthusiastic about the place, and I couldn't take her savings. She sacrificed a lot for it. Even Susan wouldn't take any money from her. Maggie's really frustrated,'' she finished with a big grin.

Paula arrived at their table with two big pieces of apple pie.

''Pie, after all that dinner?'' Will protested, but he was studying the dessert with a lot of interest. ''Maybe just a bite.''

Kate chuckled. ''If you stop after the first bite, I'll have my feelings hurt.''

''I knew you were going to be dangerous to my health,'' he teased in return. But, in truth, he was growing more and more fearful each day. Because his intense interest in everything that concerned Kate was growing out of control.

As Will finished the apple pie with a satisfied sigh that pleased her, Kate offered an apology. "I didn't mean to talk your ear off. You probably need to get back to the office. Oh! I didn't ask why you came."

Will laid down his fork and reached into his pocket, pulling out a small box. "I almost forgot. I found you a ring this morning."

Kate's breath caught in her throat. *It's only pretend,* she reminded herself. "A cubic zirconia?"

Instead of answering, he popped open the box.

Kate couldn't breathe. An incredibly large marquise diamond, flanked by two smaller matching stones, set at an angle to the larger one, shone up at her.

"Do you like it?"

"Of—of course, it's beautiful. But isn't it too large? I mean, no one will believe it's real."

"It's not that big," he returned, setting the box down and lifting out the ring. "Let me have your left hand."

Kate couldn't keep her fingers from shaking as the cool metal slid down her finger. "Is that silver?"

"No, white gold," he said in an absent manner, his gaze fixed on her finger, noting the perfect fit.

"But that's expensive. Why would they use white gold with a fake stone?"

"Do you like it?" he asked, ignoring her question.

"I told you I love it. If I make the business a success, maybe I can buy it when—when we're through.'' She stared at the beautiful ring, turning her hand first one way and then another.

He ignored that comment, too. ''I have to go back to the office, though I feel more like a nap after that delicious lunch. You start packing. I'll meet you here at about six-thirty and we'll take your things back to my house.''

''Is anything wrong?'' There was something in his tone, rather than his words, that made her think he was disturbed.

''No.'' Instead of any explanation, he slid from the booth, pulled her up beside him and wrapped her in his arms. As his lips met hers, Kate thought dazedly that this kissing thing was becoming a habit.

Then she didn't think at all.

With whirlwind activity, enough to keep her from thinking, Kate was all packed by the time she left to meet Miriam at Hall's, the prestigious store on the Plaza.

She didn't want to think about moving into Will's house. And she didn't want to think about choosing a wedding gown, either. Even the ring on her finger made concentration difficult. Though the stones weren't real, the ring still must have cost more than normal costume jewelry.

She hurried into the Bridal Shop of Hall's and discovered Miriam already in consultation with a saleslady.

''There you are, my dear. What size are you? I guessed an eight,'' Miriam said in greeting.

"Yes, I wear an eight."

"That's perfect," the saleslady enthused. "We buy our models in an eight. I'm sure we'll be able to find something for you to wear soon."

Kate nodded, finding their concern bothersome. Of course she could find something to wear in four weeks. She moved toward the racks of white gowns, but the saleslady stopped her.

"Just sit down here, and we'll show you what we have." She gestured to several sofas.

"Wouldn't it be faster if I select those I'm interested in?"

Miriam stepped forward. "Child, Agnes knows her job. Come sit with me and she'll ask about your tastes."

With a resigned sigh, Kate sat down.

The saleslady sat near them with a pad and pen and asked about the kind of dress Kate wanted.

"Simple."

The saleslady blinked several times, as if Kate had said something shocking.

"She means in elegant taste, of course. With her figure, she can wear almost any style, but she prefers the simplicity of the top designers," Miriam translated with perfect ease.

"I don't think a designer gown will be necessary," Kate said urgently to Miriam. After all, she didn't want the price of a designer gown.

Both women ignored her. "I think I know just the gown. You'll love it!" Without waiting for their approval, Agnes hurried over to the rack of dresses. She pulled down a hanger and quickly whisked away the plastic bag, then came back to them.

"Do you remember the Kennedy wedding? This gown is by the same designer. The current star in designing wedding gowns."

Kate was prepared to dismiss the gown at once, knowing it would be utterly out of her price range, but she couldn't. The lustrous satin seemed to cling to her fingers as she touched it. Simply cut with a low rounded neckline, a slender outline that flared below the hips and small cap sleeves, it was exactly the type of dress she might have dreamed of.

"You're right as always, Agnes," Miriam agreed. "Try it on, dear. You will look exquisite."

Before Kate could pull herself together enough to refuse, she found herself in a large dressing room. Oh, well, she might as well try the gown on. What could be the harm?

Except that she never wanted to take it off. Staring at herself in the mirror, Kate realized she had a very romantic streak in her. She loved the gown. Though simple in style, its cut was by a master and was flawless.

"Are you ready yet? We're quite anxious to see how it fits," Agnes called through the door.

Kate opened it and stepped back into the show-room. Both women stared at her, saying nothing.

She bit her bottom lip. Did they hate it?

"Oh, my, I guess I understand my son's fascination with you, Kathryn. I may call you Kathryn?"

"Most people call me Kate."

"But I shall call you Kathryn. So much more elegant. It matches the gown. Do you like it?"

Kathryn swallowed. She considered lying, but she couldn't bring herself to do so. The gown was too beautiful. "It's wonderful. Of course, I don't think—"

"Wonderful. We'll take it, Agnes. Just put it on my bill. Now, do we need any altering?"

"No, wait, we don't even know how expensive it is," said Kate, trying to halt the purchase. She might as well have tried to stop lava flowing from a volcano. The other two put their heads together, pushing and pulling on the gown to be sure it fit properly, ignoring her gauche comment.

As Kate reached forward to smooth down the skirt, after Agnes had twitched it, Miriam shrieked.

"What? What's wrong?" Kate asked, turning in alarm.

"William gave you a ring and you haven't told me? How could you be so cruel?" Though she clutched Kate's hand, she glared at her, as if she'd intentionally hurt her.

The saleslady stepped forward to admire the engagement ring. "Oh, my, you are a fortunate young lady. I know that ring."

"I beg your pardon?"

"My husband works at Plaza Jewelers. He's shown me that ring a dozen times. He says it's the finest diamond they've ever received. When I talked to him at noon, he was so excited because he'd just sold it. The commission was fabulous."

"I think there must be some mistake," Kate said faintly, feeling sick to her stomach.

"Oh, no, there isn't. There aren't that many twenty-five-thousand-dollar rings in the store. Besides, my husband said it was my favorite ring that he sold. And that's it. You are lucky."

"My son has exquisite taste," Miriam said proudly. "At least in rings."

Kate didn't bother to respond to the slight. She was too busy planning ways to kill William Hardison.

Chapter Nine

By the time Kate arrived back at the diner, Will had already loaded the boxes into his car. Madge had shown him where everything was.

In fact, he was feeling quite satisfied. True, this plan was taking a lot of time away from work, something he hadn't counted on. Surprisingly he didn't mind that much. At least his mother wasn't constantly exasperating him with her nagging.

Tonight, he planned a special dinner to celebrate their engagement. If it had been a normal engagement, he would have had the meal at home, candlelight for two. However, he'd made reservations for them at another restaurant on the Plaza. It wasn't that he needed to be seen with Kate. Already, he was receiving calls of congratulations. Word was spreading.

No, the problem was that he couldn't trust himself to be alone with Kate, with a bedroom just down the hall. He'd promised a platonic marriage. He hadn't even gotten to the ceremony yet, and he was already struggling with that aspect.

It scared him. He wasn't willing to trust a woman to be honest and reasonable. To love him in return. Even Kate, as loyal as she was to her father, as generous as she appeared to be, as selfless, could turn on him.

His heart protested, but his head insisted.

So they would dine in public.

Still, as he sipped a cup of coffee at the counter, he was silently patting himself on the back.

Until a redheaded whirlwind blew through the door. And continued right past him, blistering him with a glare.

"Kate?" He slid from the stool and followed her through the kitchen. Until he reached her bedroom, or what was left of it, and had the door slammed in his face.

"Kate?" he repeated, rapping softly on the door.

To his surprise, the door sprang open at once. He'd figured it would take a lot of cajoling before he faced her again.

"Where are my things?" she demanded.

"I've already loaded them."

"Bring them back."

"Kate, what's wrong?"

Without answering, she slid the ring that he'd given her at lunch off her finger, handed it to him and slammed the door again.

After staring at the ring, trying to figure out what was going on, Will couldn't hold back a smile. Life with Kathryn O'Connor was certainly interesting. He didn't have to worry about her complying with his every word.

"Kate?" he called again.

No answer.

"Kate, I'm not going away until I find out what's wrong. If my mother tried your patience, I'm sorry, but I warned you about her."

The door whipped open. "Don't you dare blame your mother!" she raged. And slammed the door again.

Well, he was narrowing down the identity of the guilty party. Namely him. He rapped on the door again. "Kate, if you'd explain, I'm sure we can work something out."

"Go away."

"I can be as stubborn as you, Kathryn O'Connor. And I have all your belongings in my possession."

The door opened a third time, much to his surprise, but he figured it would be slammed shut immediately. His most optimistic thought was that it would soon fall off its hinges at the rate Kate was going.

However, this time, the diva of the diner didn't spew venom at him and then slam the door. She charged past him and was through the kitchen before he even moved.

"Wait, Kate!" Running after her, he reached her as she was trying to lift one of the boxes out of his back seat. Instead of grabbing the box and enjoining a tug-of-war, Will seized a more enticing hold. He slid his arms around Kate's small waist and pulled her back against him.

"Kate, if you don't explain what's going on, we're

going to put on a whale of a show for all the diner patrons. They're staring out the window at us now.''

She froze, and he suspected she was staring at the rows of windows filled with the customers.

He pressed his advantage. ''In fact, I think you should turn around and kiss me. Otherwise, you're in violation of our agreement and I'll have to ask for my money back.'' He grinned, sure she'd realize he was teasing her.

Instead she slumped against him, her head falling, and muttered. ''I think that would be best.''

Now he knew he was in serious trouble. Kate wouldn't let just anything come between her and the restoration of the diner. Witness their pretend engagement.

''Honey,'' he whispered, holding her closer to him, ''tell me what's wrong. You know we don't want to tear up the agreement. It's good for both of us.''

''You lied to me.''

She stiffened against him, her hands pulling at his as they clasped her waist.

''How did I lie to you?''

''You said that ring was a cubic zirconia!''

''I didn't say it was a cubic zirconia.''

''Okay. You let me think it was a cubic zirconia. Instead it's a rare diamond you paid twenty-five thousand dollars for. That's half of what you're paying me. If I'd lost it, I couldn't—'' Her voice had begun to tremble halfway through her words and she broke off as the trembling extended to her tense body.

He snuggled closer, if it was possible, and whispered, ''Someone's got a big mouth.''

She sniffed. "Well, it certainly isn't you."

"And this is what all the fireworks were about?"

With an explosive force, she spun around, breaking free of him. "Don't you think it deserved fireworks?"

"Nope."

"I can't wear that expensive a ring! I don't—I'll lose it."

"If you do, it's insured. I'll get you another one."

"Why did you buy this one? Our engagement is a—"

His lips covered hers to stop her from announcing their relationship a sham. At least that's why he told himself he kissed her. Once their lips touched and her heat removed all trace of the crisp coolness of fall in Kansas City, he didn't care why he was kissing her.

As long as he could.

She finally broke away from him, her breathing as labored as his. "We have to s-stop."

"Right," he agreed, but his gaze remained glued on her lips, in case he saw any indication that she wanted to renew their embrace.

"Will!"

"Yeah?"

"You're not listening," she complained.

He shook his head, in an attempt to break the spell of their embrace, and said, "Okay, I'm listening now. Look, I've got dinner reservations—" he paused to check his watch "—in ten minutes. Let's get some food and talk reasonably about this situation."

At first he thought she was going to refuse, then she looked down at herself. "I should change."

"No. You look terrific."

And she did, dressed in a forest green sweater and skirt that made her eyes glow. Or maybe that had been the anger. Either way, she would draw any man's eye.

He could hardly look away.

"All right."

It took him a moment to realize she'd agreed. Then he hurriedly opened the front door and helped her in before rushing around to the driver's side. He had a fear she might change her mind and sprint for that very slammable door in the diner if he didn't.

Once they were seated in the restaurant he'd chosen and the hovering waiter had been dispensed with, he reached into his coat pocket for the ring.

Holding it in front of her, he asked, "Did you not like it?"

A flash of fire in her eyes warned him that he'd asked the wrong question. "You know I loved it!"

"Good. Listen to me, Kate. If I'd bought a cubic zirconia, the news would've run through our crowd like wildfire. Everyone would believe our engagement was as fake as the ring."

She frowned. "I hadn't thought of that. Are you sure?"

"How long did it take you to find out about the ring?"

"One afternoon, but I just happened to be waited on by the wife of the man who sold you the ring."

"Lucky me," he said with a sigh. "Honey, he's going to brag about his commission, if nothing else. But there are gossip columnists who pay for that kind of information. Word would get out."

"But it's so expensive."

"Kate, I told you it's insured. Besides, it reminded me of you."

"Why?" she asked with solemn green eyes.

"Because it's all bright and shiny and over the top."

"I'm not sure that's a compliment."

He grinned. "Oh, yeah, it's a compliment. Now, will you please take back the ring?"

"You're sure it's insured?"

"I'm sure." Reaching over for her hand, he slid the ring on her third finger, left hand, and then blinked as the flash from a camera blinded him.

"Damn!"

"Good evening, Mr. Hardison," a chirpy voice said.

When he could see, Will recognized a society reporter he'd seen at various events. "Good evening, Ms. James."

"Oh, make it Viola. We've known each other forever. But I don't think I've met your companion."

Will looked at Kate, hoping she would realize now was not the time to be difficult. "I'd like you to meet my fiancée, Kathryn O'Connor."

Kate nodded but said nothing.

"Then this is an auspicious occasion. May I see the ring?"

Will nodded when Kate looked at him, a question in her eyes. Then she extended her left hand.

"Wow! You are one lucky young woman."

"Actually I'm the lucky man," Will said hurriedly.

"Well, if you don't mind, I'll have my photographer take a picture of the two of you toasting your future. It'll make a great photo for the paper, too, but I'll send you a copy.''

They posed because Will knew that was the fastest way to be left alone. Viola had stalked him for several years, taking his photo every time he was out with a different woman. He believed his mother either paid or encouraged the reporter.

After tonight, Viola's interest in him as an available man should diminish.

The waiter brought their meal and Viola faded away.

''Does this happen to you often?'' Kate finally asked, her voice subdued.

''Actually no. I've never gotten engaged before.'' He grinned, hoping to tease her back to a smile.

''You know what I mean. Someone following you around, taking your picture when you least expect it.''

''Yeah. But in the future, they won't have any interest in me, because I'll be safely married.''

She gnawed on her bottom lip, and Will remembered its softness when he kissed her by the car. Heat coiled in his gut.

''I think I have more sympathy for you now than I did. I thought you were being a little overly dramatic about everything.''

''After meeting my mother?''

''Will, I believe you're too hard on your mother. She's really very sweet.''

''What did you say?''

''I said—''

"Never mind. I heard you. I just can't believe you said it."

"She was very nice to me this afternoon."

"Kate, she has hounded my very existence since my father died. Demanding I supply her with whatever amount of money she wants, forcing me to make public appearances, trying to marry me off to every debutante who appeared on the scene. She's made my life hell!"

"But I think that's because she's lonely."

With dramatic flair, he smacked his forehead before muttering, "I can't believe you've gone over to the enemy's side. How could you betray me like that?"

He was trying to make her laugh, but inside there was a nagging hurt that she didn't see his mother as he saw her.

Somehow, she must have sensed his deeper feelings. Reaching out to put her hand on his arm, she said, "I'm not supporting your mother's behavior, Will. I understand that it might have, er, made your life difficult. But— If you'd marry and give her some grandchildren, I think she'd be a lot happier."

He took a bite of his veal and chewed it thoroughly before he answered. "I am marrying. Want to rework the contract? One grandchild? Two? How many do you think would satisfy her? And we won't worry about how a divorce would affect our children. After all, it's part of the agreement."

His sarcastic response silenced Kate. Maybe she'd had no business advising him about his mother, but the woman increasingly seemed more pathetic than vicious.

And Will's obviously false offer to give her a child lit a flame deep within Kate. She'd already begun to think along those lines before she returned from France. Though all her energies were focused on the diner and putting herself in a position to help her family, she was more aware than ever, after Pop's death, of the frailty of life.

"Kate?"

"Yes?" She met his gaze, hoping he couldn't read anything in her gaze.

"I let my temper get away from me. I apologize."

Relief flooded her. "I don't think I can hold that minor reaction against you after my major blowup earlier."

"You mean that 10-rounder we had at the diner?" he teased, a grin on his lips.

Such a gorgeous mouth. And it could bring such magic. She dismissed those crazy thoughts. "Yes, I'm afraid so. Pop always warned me about my temper. I thought I'd done a good job of controlling it until I met you."

"It's not often I lose mine, either. Maybe we have a strange effect on each other."

She already knew that. Only it wasn't her temper she was worried about losing.

The closer they got to Will's house, the more tense Kate became. Not only did the elegance of the house intimidate her, but also the close proximity to Will's sexy body did nothing to calm her.

"Here we are," Will announced unnecessarily as he pulled under the porte cochere at the side of the house.

"I don't have my car. I'll need—"

"I'll take you to the diner in the morning, honey, and then you'll be able to come home when you're ready. I'll get you some keys made, too, though Betty is usually here."

"Does your housekeeper live in?"

"Yeah, she has her own apartment just over the garage."

But not actually in the house. If Kate left her room late at night, there would be no one to see if she returned to her own bed. Or visited anyone else's bed.

Stop that! She was determined to keep her distance. The man had no permanent plans with her. He'd been honest about the duration of their relationship. But candlelight dinners didn't help her resistance.

She'd concentrate on her family. Pop was gone now, and she was the eldest. It was up to her to be there for her family. To make up to Susan for Pop's absence in her life. She and Maggie were resolved on that.

So she had no time for William Hardison.

The minute he opened the door, she remembered the newest addition to her family. "Duke!" She swept the puppy up into her arms and beamed at Will.

"I can see you'll be a lot of help disciplining that monster."

"Don't call him names," she ordered, snuggling the wriggling puppy against her.

"Like he knows the difference." But in spite of his

words, his hand reached out to caress the puppy, who almost bent over backward to lick Will's hand.

"I can see you've cowed him with your cruelty," she said, grinning, forgetting her resolve to be distant.

"Yeah, well, he kind of gets under your skin. Until you accidentally step into a puddle he's left for a surprise."

"Oh, no! Your beautiful house. I'm so sorry, Will, I didn't think about that. We'll start paper-training him right away."

"I should've thought of that, but I've never had a puppy before."

"I'm sorry. I think every child should have a pet."

"Waking up with doggy breath in my face makes me question that sentiment."

Kate noticed he continued to stroke Duke as he complained.

"You let him sleep with you?"

"He cries. If I don't let him in bed with me, I don't get any sleep, either."

"And you were talking about *me* not being able to discipline?"

"Maybe we can learn together."

She nodded in agreement, but inside she warned herself to avoid any joint projects with William Hardison. He was too much temptation.

"Um, I need to call Maggie before it gets too late. I haven't told her that I won't be at the diner. She'll get worried."

"Of course. Let me show you your room. And I'll write down the number for you. We can have Maggie, and Susan, too, over for dinner soon, so they'll be comfortable here. I want you to treat my house as your own.''

The tension was returning. Kate followed Will up the wide staircase in the center of the house. Upstairs, he opened the second door on the right, and she slipped past him into a wide, spacious room, decorated in peach and baby blue.

"Lovely," she murmured, comparing it to the scruffy room she'd called home.

"If there's anything you don't like, we can change it. The color? Would you prefer a different color?"

"Will, it's temporary, remember?" He was making her more and more nervous.

"Of course. I didn't mean—but we can still redecorate if you want."

"No, the room is fine."

"You have your own bath," he said, pointing to a corner door by the wide, beautifully draped windows.

"How convenient."

"I'll tell Betty to be sure you have a good supply of everything."

"Will, I'll be fine."

He crossed to the bed and took a notepad from the bedside table. "Here's the number to give to Maggie." As he put it down, he moved to the door. "I'll bring up your belongings."

"Thank you." She didn't move toward the phone, which happened to be beside the bed, until he had closed the door behind him.

Only then did she call her sister.

"Maggie, have you gone to bed?"

"No, I was just getting ready to, though. It's ten o'clock."

Good old conservative Maggie.

"I tried to call you tonight. Where were you?" Maggie asked before Kate could explain the reason for her call.

"Out to dinner."

"With whom?"

"Maggie, I called for a reason. I need to give you a new number where you can reach me."

Dead silence.

Then Maggie, her voice cautious, said, "What do you mean? Aren't you at the diner?"

"No."

"I have room for you here, Kate. I don't like the idea of you wasting money on a hotel."

Kate swallowed. This conversation was more difficult than she'd envisioned it.

"I'm not at a hotel, Maggie."

"Where are you?"

"Um, I'm—I'm at my fiancé's house."

Chapter Ten

"William, I can't arrange the wedding."

In the midst of a management strategy meeting, Will couldn't indulge in a lengthy conversation with his mother. "I'm not going to argue with you about marrying Kate," he said in a low voice.

"No, you don't understand. I still don't approve of the marriage, though Kathryn is better than I thought. But I can't line up a caterer or a florist for the date you gave me. I got lucky on the engagement party because there was a cancellation, but the marriage date is impossible."

"Mother, I'm in the middle of a meeting. I'll—I'll choose an alternate date later and call you."

He tried to turn his attention back to the meeting. He was engineering a takeover of a frozen foods firm that would change the future of his company. He couldn't afford to make mistakes. But a postponement of the wedding bothered him.

He'd been sharing his house with Kate for four days. Four days of heaven and hell. He loved starting his day with a cup of coffee and Kate. Her disheveled beauty stirred him beyond belief. A rumpled Kate was sexier than any bandbox beauty he'd ever seen.

Unfortunately that attraction was also his hell. He couldn't do anything about satisfying his desire. And it needed satisfying. He told himself he wouldn't want her so much if he could look forward to sharing a bed with her. But that blasted agreement, at his insistence, made any liaison between them impossible.

"Damned idiot!" he muttered to himself.

His right-hand man, Brian Downey, halted in mid-sentence. "I beg your pardon, Will. I thought you agreed with me."

He apologized immediately. "I do. It's this damned wedding that—" he broke off, realizing he hadn't informed his management team of his imminent nuptials. It took several minutes to calm the excitement that raced through them.

"Of course I'll introduce Kate to you. You'll all receive invitations to the party Friday night. In fact, they were mailed yesterday."

"Friday night?" someone gasped. "But I was going to—but I'll be there, sir. It's just short notice."

"Please, don't change your plans on my account. I know it's short notice, but I didn't want to wait."

His cheeks burned as he realized how eager he sounded. And he would be, too, if it meant he could take Kate to his bed. He explained his mother's message.

"Too bad you can't change the engagement party

to a wedding since you've already got the caterer,'' Brian offered with a chuckle. Several men joined in the laughter, pointing out the reaction of the women present to such an outrageous suggestion.

Will brought the meeting back to its original purpose, but Brian's suggestion kept playing over and over in his mind. He wouldn't mind upsetting his mother, and in turn the rest of Kansas City society. In fact, that had been the plan all along. The only person he was concerned about was Kate.

Would she agree to marry Friday night?

As soon as his meeting was finished, he told his secretary to cancel the rest of his appointments and then he headed for the diner. All the way over, he marshaled his arguments.

The diner, closed now until the remodeling was completed, was empty of even the workers when he walked in. Only Kate was there, standing near the old counter, her face buried in her hands.

Immediately alarm kicked in. He circled her trembling shoulders with his arms. "Kate? Are you all right?''

After a week of avoiding him as much as possible, Kate leaned against him, letting him support her. He reveled in her body pressing against his, almost forgetting her distress.

"I'm fine. It's just…I want to remodel and make everything a success, but…I hate to see it change. That doesn't even make sense, does it?''

He turned her around, staring at that trembling bottom lip that always enticed him, the tears seeping from her hazel eyes. Using his knuckles to stroke away the moisture from her cheeks, he leaned down and gently rubbed her lips with his.

"Yeah, it makes sense. When Dad died, it was hard to get rid of his clothes. He'd never wear them again, but it meant I had to admit he wasn't going to be there."

She pressed her head against his shoulder. "Yes. I guess you do understand."

He held her close, giving her time to recover. And tried to ignore his body's response to her warmth.

"I have a proposal for you," he finally muttered when he didn't think he could hold her much longer without her becoming aware of his arousal.

She pushed back, more composed, and smiled at him. "You've already proposed once. Are you going to be a bigamist?"

"If it's the same bride, I don't think I can be a bigamist." And he couldn't imagine any other woman he'd want as his bride.

"Good point. Then, what's the proposal?"

"That we marry Friday night."

He pulled her back against him as her knees seemed to crumple beneath her.

"What—what did you say?"

"Let me explain. You'll see it makes sense," he assured her rather than repeat his idea. "Mother can't arrange a wedding four weeks from Friday because the caterers and florists are all booked. This Friday works because there was a cancellation."

"I don't—you think you can change it from a party to a wedding?"

"Why not? We'll surprise everyone. Halfway

through the evening, you disappear and change into the wedding gown. I'll step up and announce our wedding, the rental company can set out chairs, a minister will step forward and we'll have a wedding. We already have flowers, food, guests. What more do we need?''

Guts would be nice.

Because Kate wasn't sure she could handle Will's surprise. Four days of living with him had made her question their engagement, much less their marriage. That chemical reaction she'd already experienced when they touched was making such proximity very difficult.

And now he wanted to marry her Friday night?

"We can't. The dress won't be ready."

"Call them and offer a bonus. Tell them you need the dress early for the bridal portrait. They'll accept that excuse easily."

"But my family—"

"Will be there. Maggie and Susan are invited. And even your snobby aunt from Boston. Who else will you need? Tori will be there, too. You gave Mother a list, didn't you?"

Yes, she had, and now she regretted it. "The—the license. We wouldn't have time—"

"That's why I'm here. We can go this afternoon."

"Everyone will be shocked."

He chuckled and lifted her chin so she had to look at him. "Don't you remember? That was the real reason for the marriage in the first place. In fact, if we don't do something odd, you're going to become society's newest darling and I'll have to go to even more parties.''

He'd already accepted two invitations he'd insisted they had to attend. She would have been perfectly happy to ignore them, or at least refuse them politely.

"Haven't you ever heard of the slogan, Just Say No?" she demanded in irritation.

"Honey, I'm no happier about these parties than you are, but I don't want to insult anyone. It's a tightrope walk, but I think our surprise marriage will help out." He stroked her back as he spoke, sending tingles up and down her spine.

She pulled away. "This is crazy, Will. Maybe we should rethink—"

"What? Getting married?"

He sounded ferocious, glaring at her. She swallowed, her throat suddenly dry. "Well, it's—I'm not sure—"

"You were sure about spending my money," he growled.

She had no comeback for his accusation. After all, he was right. She'd been writing checks right and left to pay for the work done on the diner. She had no choice.

Calmly, as if her heart weren't beating impossibly fast, she said, "Yes, you're right. I'll call about my dress right now."

Moving away from him helped her breathing. She found the number for the Bridal Shop at Hall's and talked to the saleswoman. Though she protested, the woman finally agreed that the gown could be picked up Friday morning.

Kate turned around to discover Will staring at her, his arms crossed over his chest.

"That's taken care of. Shall we go get a license?" she asked, struggling to keep her voice even. Perhaps her tone was a little high, but she did the best she could.

Will didn't answer. He uncrossed his arms and waved for her to precede him. It was only after they were in the car and he was backing out of the parking lot that either of them spoke again.

"What did your mother say?"

In flat, even tones, he said, "I haven't told her. Nor anyone else. This will be our little secret," he ordered, "except for the minister. And the florist. You'll need a bridal bouquet."

"And a cake? If there's no cake, people will—"

"And a cake!" He squared his jaw as if he were gritting his teeth. "Damn it! Half the town will know by Friday night."

"Maggie, you are coming Friday night, aren't you? You and Susan?"

Silence was the response, and Kate gripped the phone tightly. "Maggie?"

"Kate, I was going to call you. Susan and I talked about it and...well, we wouldn't fit in with your guests, and neither of us has anything appropriate to wear. Would you mind terribly if we didn't come?"

Kate's eyes filled with tears. She didn't think she could go through with the plan if her sister wasn't with her. "Maggie, I—I need you there. Please."

"Okay, I'll be there," Maggie immediately said. "I'll find something to wear. But Susan—"

"Susan has to be there, too."

"Kate, it's not like this is your wedding. We'll both be there for your wedding, but—"

"Yes, it is." She wasn't supposed to tell anyone, but if it meant the difference between her two sisters being there or not, she couldn't keep the secret.

"What did you say?"

"We—we're going to get married Friday night. But it's a secret. You mustn't tell anyone."

"Why? Why the change? Are you sure you're doing this of your own free will?" Maggie's protective tones eased the tension in Kate's heart.

She gave a watery chuckle. "Yes. I certainly wrote all those checks for the work on the diner of my own free will."

"I have enough money to pay at least half of it back, if you've changed your mind. And I could probably get a loan for the rest of it."

"Maggie, I love you so. But I can't allow you to mortgage your future for something that you don't believe in. You've always hated the diner."

"Not hated, Kate. That's too strong. It just wasn't—I didn't fit there. I'm not like you and Pop."

Kate swallowed her tears. "Nope. You're better. Look at how successful you are."

Maggie broke the silence that followed. "Listen, we'll be there to support you. Is there anything I need to do for you?"

"Pick up Aunt Lorraine at the airport."

Maggie groaned. "Can't I do something else, like drive spikes in my hands or walk on shards of glass?"

"I need you to meet her. Pick up Susan first, then Aunt Lorraine and all three of you come here to dress for the party." The sooner she had her family around her, the better off she would be.

"Are you sure? We don't want to intrude."

"I need you."

"We'll be there," Maggie assured her with no more hesitation.

Thank God for family.

Will spent the next three days making secret arrangements with the caterer for a cake, with party rental people for chairs, with the florist for a wedding bouquet. He even added bridesmaid bouquets for Maggie, Susan and Tori and corsages for his mother and Lorraine Feherty.

He was going to ask Charles to be his best man, but it occurred to him that Kate didn't have anyone to give her away. Or at least escort her down the aisle.

A quiet consultation with Charles, a greatly shocked Charles, he might add, took care of that. He didn't ask any friends to be groomsmen. He would recruit them when he announced the wedding. After all, they would be in attendance.

He was so busy, in fact, that he scarcely had time to think about the event he was planning. He'd thought he'd approach the wedding date with apprehension. After all, he'd never planned to marry.

Probably the reason he wasn't shaking in his boots was that he knew the wedding wasn't real. Kate couldn't betray him. He had legal protection.

Besides, the danger in a marriage was giving one's heart. And he had no intention of doing that.

Of course, according to the legal agreement, the real danger was in taking her to his bed. If that happened, then his heart didn't matter. She could take half of everything he owned. Kate might not even realize how much she would gain, but his worth was over three hundred million.

And would be more when he took over the frozen foods company.

An entire year of not touching Kate.

His life was going to hell in a handbasket.

"William," his mother said as soon as he answered the phone on Friday morning at the office.

"Good morning, Mother."

"What are you doing at the office? I need you here."

"Where are you, Mother?"

"At your house, and neither you nor Kate are present."

"No, we're both at work. Isn't Betty there?"

"Of course she is, but she's not the one getting engaged."

He sighed. "What is the problem, Mother?"

"I thought you would be here to direct the party rental people. They've brought a lot of folding chairs. And the man was rude to me when I told him he'd made a mistake!"

Will realized he'd made a mistake if he thought he'd be able to get any work done this morning. "I'll be right there, Mother. Get Betty to make you a soothing cup of tea and don't talk to the rental people."

"Of course not! I'll just let him know that you are

on your way and he'll regret his hasty words!'' She
hung up the phone, satisfaction ringing in her voice.

It appeared the rental people would deserve a bonus
by the time he got home.

Kate didn't come back to Will's house until three.
She had trouble thinking of the house as anything but
Will's. She was only temporary, she reminded herself.

Since Maggie, Susan and Aunt Lorraine would arrive around four, she thought that would give her time
for a leisurely bath. Plenty of time.

Too much time.

She didn't want to think about what she was going
to do that night. Her heart ached at the thought and
she didn't want to ask herself why.

Fortunately she had no time to think. Nor to take
a leisurely bath. Both Will and Miriam were waiting
for her.

Will drew her aside as soon as she entered. ''The
bridal bouquet and three bridesmaid bouquets are in
your room. I thought you would want Tori as well as
your sisters to stand up with you.''

Bridesmaids? She hadn't even thought of such a
thing. All she could do was nod.

''Did you pick up your gown?''

''It's in the car. I was afraid to bring it in with your
mother here.''

''Okay. Go let her show you what she's done and
I'll sneak it up to your room.''

Kate followed his directions. She found Miriam
surveying the backyard, ordering various men to do
her bidding.

"No, I think the gazebo should be more centered. Move it forward two feet."

After several glares directed toward Miriam, the four men shifted the small latticework structure.

"Miriam, everything looks lovely." Fortunately Kate didn't have to lie to compliment her. There were flowers woven through the latticework of the gazebo. Tables and chairs were scattered around the large yard, white tablecloths fluttering in the breeze. Each table had a hurricane lamp surrounded by a ring of greenery and gardenias.

"All right. You may lay the dance floor now," Miriam ordered before turning back to Kate. "Good afternoon. I thought you were never coming home."

"I'm sorry. Am I late?"

"Most ladies would spend their day having a massage, a manicure, a pedicure and having their hair done. You obviously have been working at that—that diner. I'm afraid you'll embarrass my son in front of his friends."

"I promise I'll be ready on time," Kate said coolly, not sounding very apologetic. She felt sorry for Miriam at times, but not always. Sometimes she understood exactly how Will felt.

"Well, you'd best get started getting ready. You only have four hours."

A fairy godmother with a bad attitude.

Will got the wedding gown to Kate's room without his mother noticing because she was fussing at Kate outside. The gown was enclosed in an opaque plastic bag, so he didn't even have to threaten tradition by seeing the gown early.

He was smiling at his silly thought, as if this were a real wedding, when Kate met him on the stairs.

"Everything look okay?"

"Of course. Except for me, according to your mother. She thinks four hours won't be enough to make me presentable."

"I have faith in you," he assured her, a teasing grin on his lips. He couldn't resist pulling her against him and kissing her.

As her arms slid around his neck and she opened to him, he forgot the party, the wedding, everything but Kate. He wanted to take her straight to his bedroom, without passing Go.

The only thing that derailed his train of thought was the roar of a truck. Must be the catering truck. He almost shut off that thought, enjoying Kate a lot more than any thought of food, when a mental image of the wedding cake popped into his mind.

He pulled his lips from Kate's, his eyes widening.

"What's wrong?" she asked, her voice slurred with passion.

"The cake. We've got to keep Mother from seeing the cake. Where can we hide it?"

Kate blinked several times, remaining in his arms. Both of them seemed paralyzed by his question.

Then she answered. "I'll go tell your mother she needs to go home and get ready. You stall the caterers. They can unload everything else and make the cake the last thing."

She pulled herself from his arms and hurried down the stairs. Her plan was a good one, but he hated having their embrace interrupted.

He followed her down and turned right to go out

the front door. They had just opened the back of the van and were unloading a large piece of plywood covered with white plastic. On top sat a huge cake.

"No!" he ordered.

He shut his eyes as one of the deliverymen jumped in surprise and the plywood wobbled, then the cake. When he opened them a moment later, disaster had been avoided, but the catering staff wasn't happy.

"Are you Mr. Hardison?" a stern-looking lady asked, her uniform embroidered with Trudi's Catering.

"Yes, but you can't unload the cake yet."

"You almost caused us to drop it!" she complained, still incensed.

"I apologize for that. But could you put it back in the truck?"

"No, it has to come out first. Now, if you'll move out of the way—"

"But I don't— Okay, we'll put it in my study. Um, hurry."

"Mr. Hardison, you can't run a race with a cake this size. We'll do the best we can."

Will rushed into his study and swept the top of his desk clean. He should have planned for the cake's arrival, but there had been so much to do.

Just as they were bringing the cake through the door and Will was breathing a little easier, his mother let out a scream.

Chapter Eleven

Miriam charged forward. "You nincompoops! Not a wedding cake. This is not a wedding! Can't anyone do anything right?"

Kate grabbed her arm and held on, afraid she'd charge right into the two men carrying the cake. "Will?" she called, catching a glimpse of him over the men's shoulders. "I think it's time to let your mother in on the secret."

Her words got Miriam's attention, but the caterers were protesting her attack. The babble of voices increased as the front door, left open, was filled with Maggie, Susan and Aunt Lorraine.

Will stuck his head past the door of his study and looked at Kate, his lips quivering with laughter. "Are we having fun yet?"

Kate chuckled. His sense of humor pleased her so much. "Yes, Will, we're having fun. Now, why don't you explain things to your mother so the caterers can do their job? I'll take my family upstairs.''

As seven o'clock drew near, Kate stared at herself in the mirror. Susan had swept her hair up into an elegant knot, leaving a few curls to frame her face. Maggie had given her a manicure. Aunt Lorraine had congratulated her on marrying into such a wealthy family.

''Will I do?''

Her shaky question was answered by all three, reassuring her. She turned to smile at her family. ''Thank you for being here for me.''

''Well, this is certainly not proper etiquette, my dear, but I would never miss either of your weddings,'' Aunt Lorraine assured her. ''After all, I'm your family.''

Maggie and Kate exchanged a grin, knowing how Pop would have reacted to their aunt's statement. Then Kate reached out to squeeze Susan's hand. Her new sister was a beautiful blonde with a sweetness that made Kate love her, too.

A knock on the door interrupted them. Maggie stepped over and opened it slightly. ''Yes? Oh, Will.''

''Is everyone dressed?''

''Yes, come in.'' She stood back and Will, looking incredibly sexy in his tuxedo, entered.

Kate sucked in her breath as he moved closer to her. When he took her hand in his and carried it to his lips, she squashed the urge to wrap herself around him and offer her entire body for his kisses.

"You're beautiful, honey. More beautiful than any other woman in the world."

Kate told herself he was putting on a show for her family, and doing a darn good job of it, but her heart expanded with excitement.

"I brought you your wedding present."

She jerked her hand away from his. "But I don't have one for you. I didn't think—"

"I don't need one." He shoved a small box into her hands and waited expectantly.

She had no choice but to open it. Inside were diamond ear studs that complemented her engagement ring. Kate didn't think they were cubic zirconia this time. She knew her fiancé a little better by now.

"They're lovely," she whispered, overwhelmed.

"The perfect touch," Maggie added. "Put them on, Kate."

Kate did as she was told, knowing Maggie was right, but she was reluctant to accept them. A gift like earrings should be given in love, she stubbornly told herself, not as part of a pretense that was growing more complicated every day.

"Time to greet our guests. Ready?" Will asked, reaching out for her hand again.

She swallowed, her throat suddenly dry, looked at her sisters and aunt and finally took his hand. "Of course."

"Ladies, Kate will come up to change at eight-thirty. I assume you'll all assist her?"

"Shall we synchronize our watches?" Maggie asked flippantly, a big grin on her face.

Kate was surprised. Maggie, normally quiet,

seemed at ease with Will. Everyone laughed and moved to the door.

Time to begin the party.

Will checked his watch. Almost time. He turned slowly, looking for Kate. Ah. There she was, moving toward the house, Maggie at her side.

"Can't keep your eyes off her?" Peter Jacoby, an old friend, asked. "Can't say I blame you. She's a beauty. Her sisters aren't bad, either. Obviously a good gene pool."

Will grinned at him. He'd noticed Peter hanging around Susan much of the evening. "Glad you appreciate my taste. How do you feel about being best man?"

Peter appeared pleased. "Done. But what about Charles? I thought you two—"

"He's giving the bride away. Kate's father died about three months ago and she has no male relatives."

"I see. Well, I'd be pleased. Have you set the date yet? I'll need to mark my calendar," he said with a grin.

"No need. The date is now," Will said, appreciating his friend's stunned expression. Stepping into the gazebo, he approached the mike that had been set up there. Earlier, he'd introduced Kate to everyone in the very same spot.

"Ladies and gentlemen, may I have your attention?"

He made his brief announcement, causing an uproar of talk among their guests. His mother had pasted a brave smile on her face, the first smile he'd seen since he'd sprung his surprise on her that afternoon. She'd been sure the entire evening would be a disaster.

Instead everything had gone quite smoothly.

''Now, if you'll be patient for a few minutes, we're going to transform our engagement into a wedding.''

That was the signal for the caterers to bring out the cake and the party rental people to set up the chairs, forming an aisle on the dance floor. Will asked two other friends to join Peter as his groomsmen.

The minister stepped forward, shook hands with Will and took his position on the top step of the gazebo. Will saw Maggie wave from the door and he, in turn, nodded to the man in charge of the music.

He and his groomsmen, along with the minister, faced the door and Tori, holding her bouquet of pink roses, began to walk slowly toward them. Will drew in a deep breath.

He was getting married.

Susan appeared in Tori's wake, a trembling smile on her lips. Then Maggie stepped forward.

There was a pause and the wedding march began. Charles stood beside the door and offered his arm to Kate as she appeared in a white gown.

Will didn't pay much attention to fashion, but he knew the wedding dress made Kate look like a princess. Everyone stood and turned to look at her, and his heart swelled with pride.

A fluttering veil drifted from her head, surrounding her slim shoulders, framing her beauty. When she reached his side, he took her hand from Charles and drew her close. He could feel her fingers trembling on his arm and he squeezed her hand slightly.

She looked at him, a smile tilting the corners of her lips, but her hazel eyes were serious. And questioning. He remembered her attempt to back out of the marriage. But all he'd had to do was mention the money and she'd agreed.

His cynical thoughts helped to steady his breathing. The marriage was a business deal. He mustn't forget that.

The minister led them through the service. Will had taken care of both rings, giving his to Maggie earlier. Kate seemed surprised that he would wear a ring, but she slid it onto his finger, her fingers cold against his skin.

"Now you may kiss your bride," the minister said with a smile after the service was completed.

His bride. Will wrapped his arms around her and lowered his lips to hers. At least this part of the ceremony was rehearsed. Kissing Kate was something he did well.

The rest of the evening passed in a haze for Kate. Will kept her close to his side, his hands touching her, guiding her, holding her.

Making her want him.

They received congratulations from everyone. In fact, if Will had hoped to upset people by their surprise wedding, he'd misjudged his friends. They seemed charmed by the event. Even Miriam seemed pleased. Perhaps because she was receiving a lot of praise for organizing a wedding in three days.

Kate and Will exchanged grins when they overheard her taking credit for everything. Will pulled Kate closer and whispered into her ear, "I think my mother is enjoying herself."

"I bet you didn't think that would be her reaction to your sudden marriage," Kate teased.

"Ah, but I knew she'd come to appreciate your many attributes, honey," he returned, then kissed her neck.

She shivered and tried to move away, but he pulled her against him to dance to the slow waltz being played.

Even as they danced, people patted them on the shoulders, congratulated them and told them what a wonderful couple they made.

"Where are you going on your honeymoon?" someone asked.

Kate deferred to Will. She'd barely taken in the idea of the marriage. A honeymoon when they weren't—she couldn't even conceive such an event.

"We're going to postpone a trip," Will said easily. "We're both involved in some complicated business right now. I guess we'll honeymoon right here."

The man winked at Will. "The place doesn't matter anyway. My wife and I never got out of the hotel room until it was time to get on the plane to come home." With a chuckle, he walked away.

Kate kept her gaze on Will's shirt studs, trying to calm her breathing.

"Interesting," was Will's comment, but he pulled her closer to him, so they touched from shoulder to knee.

Interesting? That was his only comment? Kate had never considered herself to be particularly interested in sex. Her brief foray into it had not been terribly earth-shattering, but since she'd met Will Hardison, things had changed.

The craving he inspired in her was all-consuming. And frightening. She hadn't realized she could want a man that much. It was an out-of-control sensation that made her feel vulnerable. And she didn't like it.

Even now, if Will swept her into his arms and marched upstairs to his bedroom, she doubted she'd have the strength to protest. Even though she knew their—their marriage would end in one year. Will had been quite clear about that.

Was she masochistic?

Her worrying had to be put aside as guests began to depart. She was weary and glad to see that the evening was ending. But she was also concerned with what would happen when she and Will were alone.

Will stood aside and watched Kate say goodbye to her sisters and aunt. They were the last guests to depart. His mother had just left.

He added his words to Kate's, telling them how much he'd enjoyed meeting Kate's family. And he had. Maggie and Susan were delightful. Her aunt Lorraine, however, had reminded him a lot of his mother. In fact, the two women, at first competitively comparing their importance, had, by the end of the evening, appeared united in their plans for the future.

Will shuddered. That was all he needed—another

woman to push him into society. He'd have to rely on Kate to intercept Lorraine's efforts.

Kate closed the door behind her family and turned to lean against it. "It's been quite an evening."

"Yes, Mrs. Hardison, it has. But everything went well."

Her teeth settled into her bottom lip as she heard her new name on his lips. She hadn't thought about her surname changing.

"Ready for bed?" he asked.

Kate's head snapped up, and she stared at him.

"Separate beds, of course. I haven't forgotten the rules," he assured her. Indeed, he suddenly stepped back, putting several feet between them.

"Yes, of course. I have to meet the contractor at the diner tomorrow at eight." It helped to concentrate on fundamental things like redoing the diner.

"Good thing we're not indulging in a night of riotous sex then, isn't it? I'll go into the office. The party has taken a lot of my energy this week. I can make up some time."

They nodded at each other, but Kate noticed Will didn't let his gaze linger on her. She turned and headed for the stairs, hearing his footstep behind her.

How unromantic to be climbing the stairs in her wedding gown, the man she'd married following her, with no touching, no talking…nothing.

She paused at the door to her room. "Good night, Will."

A lopsided smile added to his charm. "Good night, Kate."

Their wedding night was over before it began.

* * *

Five days later, Will counted himself lucky. He'd scarcely seen Kate during that time. She worked long hours at the diner. He'd stopped by once, to discover a transformation had taken place, but she'd scarcely spoken to him.

When he'd offered to take her to lunch, she'd refused. Too busy, she'd said. But he noticed she tensed up whenever he was around.

At home, he scarcely arrived before midnight, when Kate was already in bed. He couldn't handle cozy evenings together. He was at his most susceptible then.

"Will, can I show you something?" Brian asked from the doorway.

"Sure, what is it?"

To his surprise, his senior executive stepped forward, holding a tray. On it were several dishes.

"Here's Jacko Food's latest frozen offering. I want you to taste it."

"When did you start handling product development?" Will asked, even as he popped a piece of what appeared to be crust with some topping on it into his mouth.

"My staff was interviewing employees, and this product came into the discussion. It seems the owner's daughter developed it. Everyone hates it, but they're afraid to say anything."

"So we're going to take a loss because of nepotism?"

"Unless they change the taste of it, I think we will. Did you like it?"

"No, it's terrible." He picked up the packaging, which was also on the tray, and studied it. "Snack-O-squares?"

"Everything they make has an 'o' in its name."

"So what do you suggest?"

"I thought maybe you could ask Kate."

Will's face froze, careful not to show the panic he was feeling. Consult Kate? That would involve going home at a reasonable time, spending an evening with her...not touching her. "I see. I suppose I could."

Brian grinned. "If she has any ideas, we could counter their nepotism with a little nepotism of our own."

"Right. Leave it with me, and I'll get back to you in a day or two."

When he left work that afternoon, at his regular six o'clock instead of the late nights he'd been pulling, he carefully carried a sampling of Snack-O-squares in his briefcase. There were other ways to handle this product development problem, but Brian seemed to think Kate would be the correct answer.

He saw the surprise on her face when he entered the kitchen a few minutes later.

"Hi. Not working late this evening?" she inquired.

"Sort of. How about you?"

"I was too tired to keep going, so I decided to take the night off. Besides, Betty called to let me know we've been receiving gifts. A huge load came today. She's filled up the living room and suggests we start opening them."

"Gifts?"

"Yes, I feel bad about them," Kate said. "Could

we leave them wrapped and send them back at the end of the year?'' She wore an anxious expression that made him want to reassure her. He reached for her without thinking, then abruptly drew back.

"No, I think we'd better open them. And write thank-you notes. Have you ordered any stationery?''

She stared at him. "Why would I do that?''

"It would make your life simpler. Order some thank-you notes tomorrow with our return address already printed. They'll send the bill to me.''

She grimaced but nodded.

"Have you eaten? We could go out to a restaurant—''

"Betty left something in the fridge. I told her I'd warm it up and clean up afterward. It's a chicken casserole that looks good. And I can fix a salad.''

It sounded like a cozy evening. "Great. I need some help with something, too. If you don't mind, I'll go grab a shower and change. Then I'll come down and help put supper together.''

A cold shower. It was going to be a long evening with Kate in a T-shirt and cutoffs, her sassy red curls pulled back in a ponytail that highlighted her cheekbones. And soft red lips.

Already his body was stirring, responding to her smile, her big hazel eyes. Where was his control? Okay, so he'd make it a *long* cold shower.

Twenty minutes later, he came down the stairs to find Kate had dinner ready.

"Do you mind eating in the kitchen? I've gotten used to having my dinner at the table each night.''

"No, of course not. Uh, I'm sorry I haven't been

here to eat with you. But I've been very busy." He watched her reaction, expecting pouting or complaints.

Instead she set a bowl of salad on the table and took her seat. "No problem."

They ate in silence for several minutes before he asked about the changes at the diner. She responded, telling him of the events of the day. Several times she made him laugh with her stories.

"And you? Did everything go well today?" she asked.

"Well, about two this afternoon, Brian brought me a sample of Jacko's latest product."

"What is it?"

"A Snack-O-square."

By the time she'd asked her questions and he'd tried to answer them, they'd both finished eating. And he'd relaxed. Kate was such pleasant company, in addition to being sexy as hell.

He fetched his briefcase and withdrew the package of Snack-O-squares. Kate took it, carefully reading the ingredients before she looked at the actual food. Once she'd bitten into it, she frowned, making such a comical face that Will laughed.

"Let's see, shall I guess your opinion?"

"Maybe you'd better not. But surely you won't market it?"

"It's a touchy situation. The owner's daughter created it. And she's his pride and joy. Brian wondered if you could improve on it."

He saw the spark in Kate's eyes at his request. She immediately began to brainstorm and gather supplies from the refrigerator. Enlisted as her assistant, Will stood next to her as she experimented. There were numerous taste tests, where she fed him tidbits and he, resisting the urge to draw her fingers into his mouth, sucked on them one at a time.

They finally abandoned the project—with a promise from Kate to continue working on it—so they could tackle the gifts piled in the living room.

An hour later, after producing a long list of gifts and their donors, Kate sighed. "I'm glad women's lib makes it possible for you to write half of these."

"Wait a minute. I didn't agree to anything like that."

She chuckled. "Oh, yes, you did. When you arranged a marriage to benefit you as much as me. It's not hard. I'll order the stationery tomorrow. We can each set a goal of thank-you notes for each evening."

"I'll be working late," he said abruptly.

Something in his voice, or maybe even his words, upset her for the first time that night. "Fine!" she snapped. "Write them at the office."

She jumped up, amid the pile of wrappings, and headed toward the door.

"Kate, wait!" he protested, on her heels. He caught her at the door and pulled her back toward him.

"What do you want?"

"I didn't mean to upset you. I'll do my share."

"Thank you," she said quietly, but she didn't look at him.

"What's wrong?"

"Nothing. I'm tired. I think I'll go to bed."

He checked his watch. Somehow, sitting with Kate,

laughing and opening presents, he'd lost track of time. But it was almost midnight. ''Yeah, I'll come up, too.''

He couldn't turn her loose, so he let his hand slide to hers. Starting from the room, he was surprised when she held back.

''What about the mess? We should clean—''

''That's what Betty gets paid for. She doesn't have a lot to do anyway.'' He tugged again, and Kate fell into step beside him.

The stairs had never seemed longer, as he brushed against Kate walking beside him. His skin burned every time he touched her. When they reached her door, she pulled on her hand as she said good-night.

When Will finally released her, he felt such a sense of loss it surprised him. ''Thanks for working on the Snack-O-squares,'' he muttered, watching her lips.

She gave a brief smile, then settled her teeth into her bottom lip. ''I'll do my best.''

Hunger filled him, and he touched her, tugging her closer. ''You'll do fine,'' he assured her. Then, as he'd known all along he would, he let his lips settle on hers.

Adrenaline and hunger filled him. He pulled her against him, his body aching to feel her heat as his lips devoured hers. It had been five long days since he'd kissed her. Only now did he feel alive.

She pulled back. ''Will, we can't—you know how we react to each other. This isn't wise.''

He knew only that he needed to kiss her again. To touch her all over. To feel her against him.

She didn't protest again. Her arms even came around his back, matching him touch for touch.

When he lifted her into his arms and headed down the hall to his bedroom, his lips never left hers. Past, present, future, all became a blur of sensations. He wanted her, needed her, desperately.

When he deposited her on the bed and slid on top of her, his hands moving immediately beneath her T-shirt, she touched him, too. Frantic, he ripped her shirt over her head and, with a mind of their own, his hands seemed to go to her cutoffs.

Before too long, they were both naked, teasing, tempting, tasting. And loving every minute of it. He eased himself into her, realizing with each glorious thrust that he'd never experienced such complete fulfillment, such happiness, before. She was his haven, all softness and warmth and womanly comfort.

His last thought as he drifted into sleep later was, ''Now we're married.''

Chapter Twelve

Kate lay beside Will, listening to his even breathing. After the storm that had consumed them, she found it difficult to relax.

Everything had changed.

She hadn't intended to lose control. But then, with Will, she had never had much control. Perhaps by the time they divorced, a year later, she would be able to breathe around him, resist touching him, not beg for his kisses. Maybe.

Even more frightening than her physical reaction to the man was the realization that she loved him. She'd missed him dreadfully the past few days. They talked about everything, sharing laughter and pleasure. The excitement that flickered through her veins whenever he touched her made each minute that much more pleasurable.

And when he took her in his arms, she never wanted to leave.

But she had to remember that he didn't want her love. And he didn't want her to stay. One year was all she had.

Unless she managed to change his mind.

As sleep overtook her, she snuggled next to him, vowing that she would teach him to love her.

Will woke as the sun was breaking over the eastern horizon, wondering why he was feeling so good. The answer was almost immediate as he felt Kate pressed against him.

He stared at her flushed, sleeping face in horror.

What had he done?

Damn it, he'd known he shouldn't get close to her. It was all Brian's fault. He would have continued to avoid her if it hadn't been for Brian's request.

Avoid Kate for an entire year?

He was too honest with himself to believe that he could have made it for a year without breaking down, without letting his hunger for her take over.

She stirred, snuggling into his body, and he fought the automatic response of tightening his hold. What was wrong with him? Did he think she cared about him?

Of course not. It was chemistry. Kate had already said it was. She didn't care. And neither did he!

A sickening feeling in the pit of his stomach acted like a lie detector, buzzing him with annoying accuracy. He couldn't love her. He'd vowed never to give a woman that power.

Women wanted money. Kate had accepted his proposal for that very reason. He should have known she'd do anything to get her hands on his millions. Just like his mother.

Anger rose. She had her millions now. But she sure as hell wouldn't earn that much for one night. He intended to get his money's worth.

Kate awoke to the glorious feel of Will's mouth on hers, his hands roving her body, his arousal pressed against her.

"Will," she breathed, meeting his lips as they sought hers. Within seconds, any doubts she had about their marriage, any qualms about his feelings, were washed away by the hunger and need that filled her.

Later, when he lay beside her, his breathing slowly returning to normal, she reached out to stroke his chest, loving the feel of him.

He shocked her by seizing her wrist in a tight hold and thrusting her hand away. "No need, Kate. You got what you wanted. I may require some attention for the next year, but I won't ask for more than twice a night."

She sat up on one elbow, staring down at him, her smile still in place. "What are you talking about?"

He rolled from the bed, keeping his back to her as he headed for the bathroom. "I'm talking about the millions you earned last night. I bet you're laughing at how easily I fell into my own trap."

Before she could respond, he slammed the bathroom door shut behind him.

Kate lay on the bed, her heart aching, as she real-

ized what her husband meant. He thought she'd seduced him to get his money.

His low opinion of her hurt. But even more painful
was the reminder, again, that their marriage would
end in one year. He had no interest in making their
union real, not even after last night's wonderful love-
making. In fact, if anything, he seemed more determined than ever to be rid of her.

Blindly she reached for her clothing, spread around
on the floor where Will had thrown it the night before.
With a sob, she fled the room, her belongings
clutched to her chest. She couldn't face him again.

After standing in the shower, crying her heart out,
Kate managed to pull herself together. As she stepped
out of the shower stall, reaching for the fluffy towel
hanging nearby, she heard footsteps in the hallway.
Her heart thudded in her throat.

They paused, then continued downstairs.

She remained in her room until she heard Will's
car leave half an hour later. By that time, she'd re-
packed the things that she'd put in the dresser. Many
of her boxes were stored in the garage, and she'd
leave them there for now. But she wasn't coming
back to this house, this man, this shattered dream,
ever again.

Dragging two suitcases down the stairs, she left
them by the front door. Before leaving her room,
she'd called for a taxi. Will had bought her a new car
on Monday after the wedding, saying he couldn't
have Pop's old, beat-up Chevrolet parked in his driveway. It was bringing down the tone of the neighbor-
hood, he'd joked.

She'd laughed and accepted the new car, believing him happy to be providing it.

Now she knew better.

She'd slipped into his room and left her rings and wedding gift on his dresser. She would take nothing of his with her.

"Betty, I don't believe I'll have breakfast this morning," she said, trying to sound cheerful.

"But, Kate, it's all ready."

And I'll throw up if I eat it. "Sorry." She heard the sound of a vehicle in the driveway. "I have to go now."

"But there's someone coming. If it's more gifts, you're going to have to take 'em."

"Yes, I'll see to it. And—thank you for everything, Betty." The housekeeper had been warm and accepting. Kate didn't want to leave without expressing her appreciation.

"Hey, you didn't even eat anything," Betty teased, a smile on her wrinkled face.

Kate said nothing else. She couldn't. The tears were hovering on the edge of her eyes, looking for a reason to fall. She backed out of the kitchen, opened the front door to the taxi driver and handed him her bags.

By the time he slid behind the wheel, she was sitting in the back seat, her purse clutched tightly in her lap, her eyes closed.

"Where to, lady?"

"The Lucky Charm Diner on Wornall."

"I think it's closed."

"I know."

From there she'd call Maggie to come get her. It might not keep Will from finding her in a day or two, but she needed to buy some time. To gain control of her ragged emotions. To learn not to love Will Hardison.

Her husband.

After lunch, Will struggled to concentrate on his work. The morning had been a disaster so far. He alternated between despair that he'd given in to his desire and a surge of adrenaline when he remembered the moments in Kate's arms.

He refused to allow any emotion in his thoughts of her, but hunger, pure, unadulterated sexual hunger, constantly plagued him.

"Your housekeeper is on line one," his secretary announced through the intercom.

"Betty, is something wrong?" he asked as soon as he picked up the phone. His housekeeper never called the office.

"I don't know, Will. I went upstairs to clean the bedrooms, and Kate's is empty. But her new car is in the driveway."

Anger filled him. So Kate had already taken it upon herself to move in with him? Had he asked her to? Who did she—

"And when I went to your room, I found her rings and those diamond earrings you gave her on your dresser. What should I do with them?"

Suddenly the anger disappeared, replaced by an ice-cold despair. "I'll be right there."

*   *   *

After he confirmed Betty's observations, Will stood in the bedroom where he'd twice made love to Kate, wondering what to do. The first thing, he supposed, was to talk to Kate. He knew where to find her. After all, nothing was more important to her than the diner.

When he arrived there, however, he discovered he was wrong. Kate had been there, the contractor replied, but then she'd left with another lady, a brunette.

Maggie. She was with Maggie.

He asked to use the phone. Directory Assistance refused to give him the number for Maggie O'Connor. It was unlisted.

Irritated, he called his mother. She assured him she had never received Maggie's phone number. Why did he need it? And why didn't he ask Kate?

Unwilling to answer any of those questions, he abruptly told her goodbye and hung up.

He charged back to his car, slammed the door and roared off toward the Plaza. He knew whom Kate would contact. He had no doubt of it.

In Charles's office, Will confessed what had happened. It wasn't pleasant, hearing his best friend call him an idiot.

"I know," he admitted wearily. "I was an idiot to have you draw up that agreement. And an idiot to think I could resist her."

"So what do you want me to do now?" Charles asked.

"Is there anything to *be* done?"

"We could sue for entrapment, maybe reach an out-of-court settlement. But it will still cost you a lot. Just maybe not a hundred and fifty million."

Will's mind immediately flew back to those fateful moments in front of Kate's door. She had been the one to stop. To suggest they not go any further. He had been the one to lift her into his arms and carry her to his bed.

"Will? What are you thinking about?"

His cheeks flushed, Will shook his head. "Nothing. I, uh, don't think we should claim entrapment. But we'll try to negotiate a settlement."

"Okay. Where do I reach her?"

"I don't know."

One of Charles's eyebrows soared. "Then how do you know she's gone? Maybe she's out shopping."

"She left her rings, earrings and car behind."

"No note?"

Will shook his head.

"Do you want me to hire a P.I.? Track her down?"

"I don't think that will be necessary. I'm sure she'll contact you to find out how soon she gets her money. Let me know when she does."

For two days, Kate stayed away from the diner, dealing with any problems by phone. During all that time, she remained in Maggie's small apartment, staring into space, wiping her cheeks before they became furrowed from all the tears.

What an idiot she'd been. To fall in love with a man who didn't want her. To give her heart, her body, her soul to him, knowing he'd throw everything back in her face in a year.

The second night, Maggie, having tiptoed around

her sister for the past forty-eight hours, finally asked, "What are you going to do?"

"I don't know," Kate whispered, her voice hoarse from all the crying.

"I still have my savings. Do you want to repay him? I can—"

Kate stared at her sister, her gaze troubled. "Would you forgive me if I stripped you of all your hard-earned money, Maggie? I will pay you back, I promise, but I don't know how long it will take."

Maggie hugged her. "I just want you to be happy again."

"I haven't spent all he loaned me. I'll stop work on the diner and take a job. Then—"

"No! You were right about the diner, Kate. You'll make a success of it. So don't give up your dream. Pay him my twenty-five thousand and asked for time to repay the rest. I'll work out a payment schedule. Surely he can give you a few years to repay if he has that much money."

Maggie's faith in her eased the chill that surrounded her heart, and the two of them worked out the offer Kate would make.

The next morning, Kate appeared at Tori's office, dressed in the infamous blue suit that had begun her saga with Will. When she explained what had happened and her intentions, Tori cautioned her.

"Are you sure you know what you're giving up?"

Thinking about Will and any chance of ever being with him, Kate nodded, tears pooling in her eyes again. She thought she'd cried out every ounce of water she'd had in her the last two days.

"It's a lot of money," Tori added.

"Money? You were talking about money? That doesn't matter, Tori. I don't want his money."

With a sigh but no more argument, Tori picked up the phone and called Charles's office. Her call was put through at once and, with a minimum of conversation, she had an appointment in half an hour.

"I'm going with you," Kate assured her.

"There's no need. I'm sure we can—"

"No. I want to be sure Charles understands."

Tori nodded in agreement, accepting Kate's decision.

Will stood by Charles's window, staring out at the sunny fall day. When Charles had called him half an hour ago to tell him Tori Herring was on her way over, Will had dropped everything and rushed to his friend's office.

The tension in him was growing every minute as they waited for Tori's arrival.

"You realize this could get ugly," Charles said. "Just let me do the talking. Tori's not an idiot, and they've got the upper hand here."

"I know. Do you think Kate will come?"

"There's no reason for her to. I'm not even sure why you're here. Don't you trust me?"

"Yeah, I—"

"Mr. Wilson, Miss Herring is here," his secretary's voice said through the intercom.

"Thank you. Send her in." Charles stood, facing the door, and Will turned, too.

He'd spent two miserable days wondering where

she was, if she was all right, if she hated him. He
wanted to know what she intended to do, and how
much it was going to cost him.

He wanted to know if he could resist her even now.

His last question was answered when the door
opened and Kate followed Tori into the office. His
gaze greedily roved over her, noting the circles beneath her eyes, her drooping lips. She wasn't happy.

Charles greeted the women, but it wasn't until Will
stepped forward that Kate realized he was present.
Her face paled so drastically, he was afraid she'd
faint.

Tori and Charles forced Kate into a chair, and Tori
pushed her head forward.

"My client didn't intend to alarm you, Kate,"
Charles said, shooting a warning stare at Will.

She raised her head, staring at Charles. "No, of
course not."

Will wanted her to look at him. He wanted her to
show him how she felt. He wanted to read avarice in
her gaze, to stop his heart from racing. To stop his
body from wanting to reach out to her. To convince
himself he didn't love her.

She didn't look his way.

There was an awkward silence, then both attorneys
began to speak.

Charles nodded to Tori. "Ladies first."

She drew a deep breath and said, "We're here
about the prenuptial agreement."

Will surprised them all, himself included, when he
muttered, "Big surprise."

With a frown at Will, Charles said smoothly, "Of

course. We were expecting you to contact us. Now I know my client signed the agreement with every intention of following it. However, I think, in light of the, uh, circumstances, you might consider a lesser award.''

Tori exchanged a look with Kate.

But it was Kate who spoke. ''What circumstances?''

Will froze. He'd told Charles not even to imply that Kate had seduced him. Surely he wouldn't—

''I'm assuming what occurred was mutual, Kate. One hundred and fifty million dollars seems a bit excessive for a little fun.''

Kate paled again, and Tori protested. ''Your client signed the agreement.''

There it was. There was the bid for his money. Now he could hate her without a qualm. Couldn't he? Why wasn't he angry with her? Why couldn't he walk out and leave the disgusting, money-grubbing negotiations to his lawyer?

''Agreed. But—'' Charles began, a smile on his lips, charm in his voice.

Tori was having none of it. She slapped a check down on the desk. ''You're under a misapprehension, Mr. Wilson. My client doesn't want Mr. Hardison's money. She's offering a check for twenty-five thousand and a payment schedule for the other half. All she asks is Mr. Hardison's leniency in allowing her to pay off her debt.''

Both women kept their gazes pinned to a stunned Charles. Will stared at them, unable to believe what he'd heard.

"I beg your pardon? Did I understand you correctly?" the lawyer finally asked.

"You did," Tori told him, her shoulders rigid.

He looked at Kate. "You're giving up your claim to Will's money? I mean, I don't want to be crass, but that's a lot of money."

"I have no claim to his money," she said, her voice even, with no inflection.

"But he said—"

"I don't know what he said, but there's no reason for me to claim his assets. I simply want to nullify the agreement...and apologize for any inconvenience."

Will frowned. Didn't she remember what she'd signed? "Kate, you know you have a right to my money."

"No, I don't."

"Are you denying what happened between us?" he demanded, outraged that she could pretend they hadn't made love.

"Will, whose side are you on?" Charles demanded urgently.

She wouldn't look at him. Only at his lawyer. "If your client will consider my offer, I'd be grateful."

"Under the circumstances," Tori added, "I think it's more than generous."

"What about the dresses, your jewelry, the car? Don't you want them?" Will demanded, stepping forward.

Kate almost shrank in her chair, angering him even more. Continuing to stare at Charles, she said, "Those things don't belong to me."

"I gave them to you, damn it!" he roared, bending over to seize the arms of her chair, staring into her eyes.

"Please instruct your client to restrain himself," Tori ordered, leaning protectively toward Kate.

"Will, please, back off," Charles asked, rising from his chair.

Unable to stare any longer into her stoic face without touching her, tracing her lips, smoothing her cheek, Will jerked away and paced toward the window.

"Perhaps we should leave the agreement with you. You can contact me in a day or two with your client's response," Tori said hurriedly, standing and pulling Kate up with her. "Thank you for your time."

"Tori, wait," Charles called, hurrying around his desk.

Will bumped into him as he raced to stop Kate's departure.

The two women almost reached the door in the confusion, but Will grabbed Kate's arm as Tori took hold of the doorknob.

"Kate, what are you doing?" he demanded, his voice raw.

"Turn my client loose!" Tori ordered.

"Tori, he's not going to hurt her," Charles protested.

Kate closed her eyes and turned away, as far as she could with Will holding on to her.

"I want to speak to my wife alone!"

Those words made her look at him for the first time since she'd realized he was in the office.

"No," she whispered, pain and pleading in that one word.

"Will, I don't think—" Charles began.

"My client doesn't want—"

"I won't sign the agreement unless I have a moment alone with her."

"Are you crazy, man?" Charles demanded. "She's offering you a way out."

Will stared at Kate's hazel eyes, her trembling lips. "Either talk to me, now, Kate, alone, or you're going to be a very wealthy woman."

Charles groaned, but Will wasn't worried. He'd finally discovered the truth about Kate O'Connor Hardison. And about himself.

He could see her gathering her strength, her courage, before she actually signaled her agreement with a nod. Without ever taking his gaze from her, he motioned to Charles to take Tori and leave.

"Kate, are you sure?" Tori asked anxiously.

Again she nodded, her gaze remaining locked with Will's.

The door closed softly behind the two attorneys, leaving them alone. Will let out the breath he'd been holding.

"Thank you."

She swallowed convulsively and nodded but said nothing.

"Why?"

Kate didn't answer right away, but she continued to stare at him. Finally she said, "I don't want your money."

"But you came to me to get money," he reminded her.

"I came to—to get a loan, or a grant. Not a handout. Not to trick you into anything."

"The agreement was my idea."

She turned her back on him. "And a wise one."

"Then why not make me pay?"

She stepped away from him, her trembling fingers clutching the back of one of the chairs she and Tori had occupied.

"Please, Will, accept my agreement. I promise I'll pay all the money back."

"Is this Maggie's savings?"

She nodded.

"I can't take Maggie's savings from her, Kate. You should know that."

Her shoulders slumped. "Then I'll give you what I have left. It's almost twenty thousand, and we'll add the rest to the payment schedule."

"You'd give up your dream? You'd stop work on the diner?"

Suddenly she whirled around, anger sparking in her hazel eyes. "What do you want from me, Will? I don't have any other choice. If you have a better plan, let me know!"

"I've never known a woman who'd choose poverty and a payment plan over a fortune."

"This isn't doing any good," she snapped, and turned toward the door.

Will stepped in front of her. His heart was singing as he realized what a treasure he'd discovered. As he realized how wealthy he suddenly was. If he had no money left, not a penny, he'd still be rich beyond his wildest dreams.

"Kate, it's doing my heart a world of good. Feel." He reached for one slender hand and placed it against his chest. She tried to escape his hold, but he couldn't allow that.

"Will, don't, please. I can't take much more." The heart-wringing plea in her words moved him.

Pulling her against him, he whispered, "Neither can I." Then his lips covered hers, and he kissed her more soundly and sweetly than she'd ever been kissed in her life, again and again taking her mouth and molding it to his, wrapping his arms around her, pressing her body to his until they almost became one, throbbing and pulsing against each other.

He finally stopped kissing her long enough to say, "I've missed you so much, Mrs. Hardison. Please say you'll come back home. I need you."

He would have returned to the business of kissing, believing he'd already discovered her answer in her lips, but she put her hand between them.

"For how long?"

Her words stopped him, and he stared down at her. "What?"

"Our agreement is for a year. I can't come back to you, Will, with that hanging over my head."

He buried his face in her neck. "We'll rip it up. I want you for my wife for all time. Kate O'Connor, will you marry me? I'll thee endow with all my worldly goods."

Kate's eyes were filled with tears again, but he prayed that this time they were happy ones.

"Just give me your heart, Will. That's the only thing I'm asking for."

"Done, Mrs. Hardison. It's been yours for quite a while now."

He returned to the kissing, which removed any possible doubt of his love.

And Kate kissed him back, pledging her own devotion as they brought each other to ecstasy.

Epilogue

"Your timing is off, Kathryn," Miriam protested. "The party at the Kavanaughs is very important."

Kate smiled wearily, not surprised by her mother-in-law's words. Miriam was all business when it came to her party-planning company.

"Don't worry. The sauces are already prepared and frozen and my assistant can handle everything else."

"Oh, good," Miriam said, consulting a list she carried with her everywhere.

"Mother, aren't you even going to congratulate Kate on such a fine job of providing you with a grandson?" Will asked, taking his wife's hand in his.

Miriam looked surprised. "Well, of course she did a fine job. Kathyrn is most competent. Now, I'll be on my way. But I'll check with you tomorrow about our schedule."

Will smiled at Kate after the door closed behind

his mother. "Didn't I warn you how difficult my mother is the first time I met you?"

"Yes, you did. But you have to admit she hasn't bothered you about your social schedule since we married."

"Nope. She's been too busy planning parties for the entire city."

"And she's been most generous about using my catering firm."

"Generous, hell. You're the best there is." He gave her a congratulatory kiss. "You'd better get some sleep before the miracle you produced wakes up and wants to be fed."

She smiled at him and they both looked at the crib on the other side of the bed. "He's wonderful, isn't he?"

He kissed her again. "Yeah," he agreed, his voice husky. "Almost as wonderful as his mother."

Will thought back to a year ago, when Kate had first burst in upon his world. He'd been bitter and lonely, sure to remain so. But Kate, in her determination to take care of her family, to create a living memorial to her father, had brought him a greater happiness than he'd ever known existed.

"Sleep tight, Kate. I'm going to miss you tonight, but Duke and I will manage on our own. I'll be back at breakfast time in the morning."

"You mean you're going to miss having a beach ball in bed with you, taking up space," she teased.

"No," he disagreed solemnly. "I'm going to miss my Kate. I don't like to let you out of my sight, but for the sake of Nathan William Hardison, our brand-new son, I'll spare you one night.'' He kissed her again. And felt his arousal stir.

"Damn it, Kate, if I don't go soon, I'm going to crawl in that bed with you, and shock the hell out of the nurses.''

She kissed him again, then pushed him away. "Go. Do all your work tonight so that you don't even think of the office for at least a week.''

"Agreed.''

From being all-consumed by his work, Will had spent a lot of time at home this past year. With Kate. And now they'd have baby Nathan to share. And if God blessed them, more children in the future.

All because he'd gotten up the nerve to marry Kate. And keep her.

*   *   *   *   *

This March Silhouette is proud to present

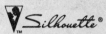
Silhouette®

SENSATIONAL

MAGGIE SHAYNE
BARBARA BOSWELL
SUSAN MALLERY
MARIE FERRARELLA

This is a special collection of four complete novels for one low price, featuring a novel from each line: Silhouette Intimate Moments, Silhouette Desire, Silhouette Special Edition and Silhouette Romance.

Available at your favorite retail outlet.

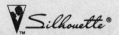
Silhouette®

FOLLOW THAT BABY...

the fabulous cross-line series featuring the infamously wealthy Wentworth family...continues with:

THE MERCENARY AND THE NEW MOM

by **Merline Lovelace**

(Intimate Moments, 2/99)

No sooner does Sabrina Jensen's water break than she's finally found by the presumed-dead father of her baby: Jack Wentworth. But their family reunion is put on hold when Jack's past catches up with them....

Available at your favorite retail outlet, only from

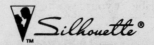

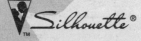

COMING NEXT MONTH

#1348 THE NIGHT BEFORE BABY—Karen Rose Smith
Loving the Boss

The rumors were true! Single gal Olivia McGovern was pregnant, and dashing Lucas Hunter was the father-to-be. So the honorable lawyer offered to marry Olivia for the baby's sake. But time spent in Olivia's loving arms had her boss looking for more than just "honor" from his wedded wife!

#1349 A VOW, A RING, A BABY SWING—Teresa Southwick
Bundles of Joy

Pregnant and alone, Rosie Marchetti had just been stood up at the altar. So family friend Steve Schafer stepped up the aisle and married her. And although Steve thought he wasn't good enough for the shy beauty, she was out to convince him that this family was meant to be....

#1350 BABY IN HER ARMS—Judy Christenberry
Lucky Charm Sisters

Josh McKinney had found his infant girl. Now he had to find a baby expert—quick! So he convinced charming Maggie O'Connor to take care of little Ginny. But the more time Josh spent with his temporary family, the more he wanted to make Maggie his real wife....

#1351 NEVER TOO LATE FOR LOVE—Marie Ferrarella
Like Mother, Like Daughter

CEO Bruce Reed thought his life was full—until he met the flirtatious Margo McCloud at his son's wedding. Her sultry voice permeated his dreams, and he wondered if his son had the right idea about marriage. But could he convince Margo that it wasn't too late for their love?

#1352 MR. RIGHT NEXT DOOR—Arlene James
He's My Hero

Morgan Holt was everything Denise Jenkins thought a hero should be—smart, sexy, intelligent—and he had swooped to her rescue by pretending to be her beloved. But if Morgan was busy saving Denise, who was going to save Morgan's heart from *her* once their romance turned real?

#1353 A FAMILY FOR THE SHERIFF—Elyssa Henry
Family Matters

Fall for a sheriff? Never! Maria Lightner had been hurt by doing that once before. But when lawman Joe Roberts strolled into her life, Maria took another look. And even though her head said he was wrong, her heart was telling her something altogether different....